I0586795

Zodiac Saga 1

The Search for the Temple Friends Foes and Zodians

Kaitlyn McKnight

Zodiac Saga 1

Copyright © 2016 by Kaitlyn McKnight All Rights Reserved.

All rights reserved. No part of this publication may be reproduced, stored in a retrieval system or transmitted in any form by any means, electronic, mechanical, photocopy, recording or otherwise, without the prior written permission of the author and publisher. This book is a work of fiction. Names, characters, places, and incidents are either products of the author's imagination or are used fictitiously, and any resemblance to actual persons, living or dead, business establishments, events, or locales is entirely coincidental.

McKnight Publishing Group PO Box 10465 Gulfport MS 39503

Library of Congress Control Number: 2016903011
ISBN-13: 978-0-9894894-2-3
Second Edition

Printed in the United States of America

Acknowledgments

Zodiac Saga 1 is dedicated to my big sister Ashley. Without her curiosity, this story would not have been shared. I love you for your continuous support and nosiness. Special thank you to my parents, my Aunt Rev. Dr. C.R.M. Moore and the Redeemed Temple Church Columbia South Carolina. For all your love, prayers, guidance, sacrifices, dedication, and encouragement. You are the best family in the world.

Origin of the Story

In the year 32 B.C.E., Aries, The Zodian god of Death, had a vision of a malevolent entity. It was evident that the entity would enslave the world and eventually destroy everything. When this news reached the other Zodians, they each stored a portion of their powers into Gems. The Temple of Zodia was built to store the Gems until the dark day came. The Elders of Zodia thought it was essential to find the entity and destroy it before the vision took place. So they each disguised themselves and lived among mortals on earth. But they became distracted with earthly pleasures. Cancer, The Zodian god of Intellect, found himself wandering in the Temple of Zodia. He made an unknown but fatal error and caused the Temple to collapse. This collapse caused the Gems to scatter and become lost. Cancer was indefinitely banished from the Temple of Zodia. The other eleven Zodians built another Temple on earth, but hid its location from mortals and Cancer. Several centuries later in the current year, a bullied 12-year-old little boy named Cyrus O'Hara believes in the existence of Zodiac gods. This belief becomes a reality for Cyrus as he sets out on an adventurous journey to find the Zodiac gods and the Temple of Zodia. Along the journey he learns the true meaning of family, friends, and foes as his true identity is discovered.

HAPPY READING!

Table of Contents

My First Magical Watch

"Cyrus hurry-up or you'll be late for school again." Peter called.

My brother Peter was a nice person; however, you couldn't tell by his appearance. He stood almost seven feet tall and had light facial hair. He had the physique of an oversized body builder with bulging biceps from intense weightlifting. He had extremely dark brown hair highlighted by his orange and brown eyes that he kept hidden behind sunglasses. Peter has a big heart and a smile that could brighten anyone's day.

"Cyrus!"

"I'm coming!" I said walking down the stairs. I had my backpack in my hand swinging it around. "Do you really think I want to go to school? Everyone makes fun of me."

"Not everyone at school makes fun of you." Peter said smiling. He put my backpack on my back.

"Yeah they do," I rolled my eyes. I hated saying that, but it was true.

"Sofia doesn't." Peter patted me on the head trying to tidy my hair.

"Yeah but just her. Everyone else does." I fixed my hair back to the sloppy mess it was.

Peter pulled a comb from his jeans pocket and handed it to me. "Just remember that I'm here for you, bro. Better things will happen soon, trust me. Now get going."

I took the comb from him and combed my hair. "Whatever you say." I lived in a small town called Callisto. It was a rural area with a low population and very little businesses. There are a few neighborhoods, small retail stores, a diner, and many farms.

There are two schools - Calibri and Garamond. The two schools are across from each other, but they are different. Calibri was a private school built for the rich and Garamond was a public school built for the poor and… well, the poor.

Of course, I went to Garamond but not by choice. Calibri was an impeccable school and probably the greatest thing that happened to the small town of Callisto. Calibri had education and Garamond had potential for education.

As I walked passed Calibri, the students were just arriving. Their Mercedes Benz's and BMW's would pull up to drop them off and then drive off at top speed. The students would be texting on their IPhones and talking to their friends at the same time. I felt like punching each of them, but I didn't because as Peter would say, "You can't just punch your anger or frustration away." Even though sometimes you would like to try.

I walked up the creaking stairs to Garamond. Not to my surprise, Judas Vince was waiting to pound my face... again. Judas was the bully at school. He always wore a blue and green ski hat that covered his head so no one could see his hair. His crimson eyes made me think about blood and gore that could destroy your happiness. The worst part about him was his pale ghostly skin.

There were always two other guys with him, Connor and Collin Fettler. They were twins but they would not tell you who was older. They both had blonde hair and blue eyes. They were the same height and always dressed alike. The only way you could tell them apart was by their voices. Connor's voice was deep and Collin's was high. I don't know why, but they

3

admired Judas a lot. Go figure. My guess is because they didn't want to get black eyes and bloody noses.

"Good morning O'Hara!" Judas said, like a person who just won a million dollars on a game show. He walked over to me and pulled my shirt toward him. "Ready for your daily beating?"

I swallowed my fear and tried not to seem scared. "Back off, Vince."

Connor laughed. "You know, for a loser who's scared, you sound kind of brave."

Collin raised his hand and hesitated as if he needed permission. Connor rolled his eyes.

"Just say it, Collin." Collin did a big smile and laugh strangely.

"Okay, okay. What we should do is tie the dork up in chains and turn him into a piñata. Just saying."

Judas looked at him. "Alright Collin, we'll go with your idea this time. Considering all your other ideas are usually useless. Besides, I've wanted to beat him with a bat anyway." Judas looked at me. "But of course before we do that, I'm going to punch him."

He raised his fist but before he could punch me, a girl walked up. It was none other than Sofia Ferguson. She had light brown hair and violet eyes that made her stand out from everyone else. She was smart and beautiful, but had a horrible temper.

She looked at me and rolled her eyes. Her voice sounded like a thousand violins. "You guys are stupid."

Judas laughed. "Whatever."

Connor and Collin laughed then looked at Sofia and in unison said, "Some friend you got there, O'Hara."

Sofia looked at the twins then Judas. "Listen Vince put him down or I'll-"

Judas laughed again. "-Or you'll what?"

Sofia looked at Conner.

He looked at her the same way. "What, Ferguson? You got something to say to me?"

Sofia did a wicked smile. She picked Connor up in the air and threw him through the doors of the school. You could hear the sound of him hitting the ground. It sounded like a bullet hitting a metal wall.

Sofia looked at Judas. "Put him down, or I'll do worse to you."

Collin looked at Judas. "Do as she says, dude!" He ducked down and put his hands on his head. "She's stronger than we thought!"

"Fine." Judas dropped me on the ground. "Next time, O'Hara…next time." Judas dragged Collin into the building.

I smiled at Sofia. "Thanks." She helped me up, but immediately punched me in the face.

"That's for making me have to save you … again! Honestly, Cyrus when will you learn?"

"Sorry." I said trying to get back up.

"I owe you one… again."

"Whatever. Let us just get to class. You know I hate being late."

I have to be honest; the worst part of school besides Judas is class. The only class I actually pay attention in is geography. Just so I could find where the Temple of Zodia is located. However, we have yet to talk about it. I wonder why.

"Mr. O'Hara, answer my question now!" Mr. Daster said. "Well?" Mr. Daster was an old man who no one liked. Not even the other teachers. He taught our math class and made it more boring than it should have been. On the other hand, maybe it was just me. He was like sixty years old and had gray hair dyed brown, but you could still see some of the gray hairs.

He wore suits that looked like they were from the 70's. The suits were complemented with bowties.

The worst part was trying to look at him in his dark green eyes. "Mr. O'Hara I will ask you one more time - what does pi equal?"

As always I had absolutely no idea what he was talking about so I just guessed. "Um.... pumpkin?" Everyone started laughing except for Mr. Daster and Sofia.

Sofia glanced at me and shook her head.

Mr. Daster walked up to my desk and looked me straight in the eyes. "Everyone may think you're funny, but I don't."

"I'm sorry Mr. Daster." I lied. "I just thought that you were talking about the pie that you eat and not the mathematical pi. Whatever it is."

Mr. Daster looked at me disgusted. "Well, Mr. O'Hara, since you think it's so funny you have a week of...." He didn't get to finish because Sofia saved me... again.

"3.14," she said, without interest.

Mr. Daster looked at her. He opened his mouth to say something, but did not get the chance.

The bell rang and I ran for the door as fast as I could. After searching through my messy locker for my geography book, I jogged through the hallway to get to my favorite class. When I reached the corner, someone pulled my arm.

It was Judas and he didn't look happy. "You're going down, O'Hara. Collin you got the chain?"

Collin looked at me as if he felt sorry for giving the idea. "Yeah…. yeah I got it."

"And I got the bats." Conner walked up with three baseball bats. One in each hand. For the third one, he had it duck taped to his back. "I found the perfect location to beat the crud out of him."

I tried my best not to scream for help. "Hey guys, just letting you know that it's illegal to do what you're about to do to me."

They all looked at me strangely. "So what?" The three of them said in unison. I looked away from them and saw Sofia.

She was looking down the hallway toward us. I was hoping she was going to save me, but instead she walked off. I didn't blame her.

Judas started to laugh. "Looks like your friend finally gave up on you, O'Hara. I know I would."

It only took a couple of minutes to get the chain around me. I was chained from my neck to my ankles.

"Guys, don't do this to me! I mean seriously Judas! I'm sure you can find a better way to hurt me. So why not just stop this? Come on guys, cut it out!"

They dragged me on my back through the hallway. We were a few feet from the main doors.

Connor laughed, "You twerp! You are not the boss of us. No one is!"

"Well *I* am."

We all looked back. From the shadows of the hallway came a tall man, our geography teacher Mr. Cazzner.

He was young with dirty blonde hair. His brown eyes showed through his thin silver framed glasses. He always wore odd colored suits and shoes to match. I looked behind him and saw a silhouette. I could not make out who it was, but I'm pretty sure I knew who would help me.

Mr. Cazzner looked at me covered in chains. "Collin, Connor, and Judas - you boys are in big trouble. To the principal's office, now!"

The three walked away with their heads down. I could not help but laugh, so I did. Mr. Cazzner helped me up and started to unchain me.

"I would warn you not to laugh, Cyrus."

"Um, sorry." I said. "It's just good to know that Judas and his followers are finally getting in trouble. And it's all thanks to Sofia." I mumbled.

Mr. Cazzner looked at me disturbingly. "Sofia didn't come to me, Cyrus."

I looked at him the same way he looked at me. "I saw a shadow behind you." I looked behind him again and still saw the silhouette. "See, its right there."

When he turned and looked, the silhouette was completely gone. It went away in the blink of an eye.

He looked back at me and sighed deeply. "Cyrus, I don't know what you saw, but I do know that if it was there, it's not anymore. Also, the only reason I found you was because you're never late for my class. That's when I knew something must have happened."

"Yeah but… I saw it. Whatever it was."

"Cyrus, just get to my class and tell them to read the first ten pages of the new chapter. I will get to class when I can. Until I get back you're in charge, so get going."

I told everyone what Mr. Cazzner said. They all sighed, so I told them to read all the pages and then they can play around. That made them all start reading. I sat in Mr. Cazzner's black leather chair and looked around the classroom. There she was, sitting in the very back of the room with no one around her. I knew the shadow had to have been her, but something told me to make sure. So I called her to the desk. Although I probably should not have called her up. "Um… Sofia, can… can I talk to you outside?"

Everyone in the class started laughing. She gave the heart stopping look she always gave me when I said or did something stupid. One of the students had to make things worse for the "Zodiac Kid", (that was my nickname at school, although I hated it.)

"Hey Zodiac Kid, are you going to give her a present, or a…"

"Enough!" Sofia yelled. "Cyrus, he's in trouble."

I looked around at the class. "Who's 'he'?"

She rolled her eyes. "Let's go, O'Hara!" She pulled me out of the chair.

The next thing I knew I was being dragged through the hallway again. Only this time I wasn't chained up.

"Where are we going?" I asked.

"Do you remember that shadow you saw?" She asked.

"Yeah," I thought about it. "It *was* you!"

"Of course it was me, dummy!" She squeezed my wrist.

"Well you don't have to yell!" I yelled back.

"Look you've noticed my eyes before right?"

"Yeah, What about them?"

"Well your belief in that story of Zodiac Saga is true. I have the Gemini Gem, which is purple."

"Which is the color of your eyes." I added on.

"The wielder of the gem can cast silhouettes any-where and make the shadow go into people and control them, right?"

"Right," she said.

"So you took control of Mr. Cazzner, right?" I asked.

"No, he told you the truth." She let go of my wrist. "I was just watching him to make sure he didn't try to take Judas's powers or-"

"Judas!" I snapped my fingers. "Let me guess his eyes are crimson so he has the Aries Gem, which is red.

That is also the color of his eyes. How could I have not thought about this before?"

"Because, I made sure you didn't until now."

"Wait, what?" I was shocked at that.

She did not respond so I moved on.

"Hold on, do we have to save Judas from Mr. Cazzner?"

"Yep."

"I don't understand, Mr. Cazzner is so nice."

"Exactly! He knew Judas and his friends always bullied you, so he paid Collin to give the idea of the piñata thing and…" she stopped and looked around.

"…and he knew I would be there to watch when they made their move. Now he knows we're coming."

"Well, even though he knows we're coming, that doesn't mean he knows the strategies we'll have," I told her.

"Let's get going." She resumed running.

"So what exactly is Mr. Cazzner going to do with Judas?" I said running behind her.

Sofia sighed. "He's going to take Judas's eye-balls out of his head. When he is done with Judas… I'm next."

"What? He is going to do what?"

"Cyrus, quiet down!" She hit me on my head. "In case you've somehow forgotten, we're supposed to be in class."

"I know. I'm sorry it's just..."

"Shhh, we're here."

Directly in front of us was the principal's office. I've been in the principal's office before and trust me, Principal Cole was one mean guy. Not that he was worse than Mr. Daster or anything.

"Okay, strategy time. We should first..." Before I could finish Sofia literally kicked down the door and ran in.

"Where's Judas?" She asked. I ran in behind her. Mr. Cazzner turned around.

"You two are just in time to watch me put an end to him."

I could see Judas bound in Principal Cole's chair. Except Judas was not tied up in a rope or chain, but somehow... metal. His hat was gone so you were able to see his hair. By surprise, his hair was snow-white. And I mean snow-white as in white hair. And I was pretty sure he didn't dye it that color.

"What do you mean 'put an end to him'?" I asked as if I did not already know. I just wanted to be sure.

14

Cazzner laughed. "His eyes are the Aries Gem which you all are well aware of. I'm just going to pull his eyes out of its socket."

"Told you." Sofia whispered to me.

"What!" Judas looked at Sofia. "I got four words for you Sofia… I TOLD YOU SO!"

Sofia shrugged her shoulders. "Whatever."

"Enough," Mr. Cazzner said. He held out his hands toward Sofia and me.

Somehow metal shot out of his hands. The metal was so powerful it slammed me up against the wall and the back of my head started to bleed. I looked over at Sofia who was on her back lying on the ground. Metal spikes were about one foot away from piercing her to death.

Cazzner laughed. "If I see your silhouette even twitch, you are through." He turned to me. "Oh yes, Mr. O'Hara. I almost forgot to tell you; at the rate of blood you're losing you'll be dead in approximately ten minutes."

I tried to call him a jerk, but instead I said, "Jec."

"I believe you meant 'jerk' Mr. O'Hara," Mr. Cazzner said with a menacing smile. "By the way before you die

I would like for you to see Azznic. I am sure you have heard of it. And if not, then be kind and say hello."

Mr. Cazzner took off his glasses and started to transform into a strange thing. I did not know if I was hallucinating or not, but to me he looked like a metal monster. His back had metal spikes sticking out, his head had rusted metal hair, and his fingers were claws. I could not really see any other parts of his body, but I was pretty sure it was bad. He walked over to me. As he walked, his body squeaked.

His voice sounded like a knife on a cutting board. "You see Mr. O'Hara I have the Aquarius Gem which gives the wielder the power of magnetism."

He looked over at Sofia who was still lying on the ground. "Now Cyrus O'Hara before you die I would like you to witness your friend's death!" He raised the spikes above her and was about to kill her when we heard a big CRAAASH from the window.

Two strange things jumped through the window. They both looked like skeletons or zombies. One was wearing a light brown torn suit with a sign that said, FEED ME. The other wore a pink dress that was also torn with a sign that read, I AM WITH STUPID.

They both threw the signs out the window and stared around the room. The one in the dress jumped over to where Sofia was and moved all the spikes away from her. As the spikes were moved, they pierced the thing in the pink dress. But to my amazement, the spikes did not even leave a mark on it. The other one ripped me up off the wall.

I did not know how it could pull off solid metal. The skeleton pulled out an old worn out bandage and wrapped it around my head. When it was done wrapping my head, it felt much better.

The skeleton in the dress turned and started fighting Mr. Cazzner, or Azznic. The skeleton by me jumped over to help the other one fight Azznic. By that time, I was totally confused.

"No get away!" Azznic said in fear. "Away!" He jumped out of the broken window and started to run away.

The two skeletons walked over to Judas and tore the metal off him. I went over to Sofia and helped her up.

"What are those things?" I asked pointing at the skeletons. "Zombies?"

"Don't call them names!" Judas said getting up from the chair. "And yes, they are zombies or skeletons." He pointed to the one wearing the dress. "This is Gertrude, the other one is Garner. The Aries Gem gives the wielder power over the dead. That's also why I look so ghoulish."

I looked over at Sofia. "You knew about this the whole time and didn't tell me? Why?"

Sofia looked down. "I thought it would be best not to tell you since…" Before she could finish, Azznic jumped back through the window and shot a spike straight toward me.

Judas swiftly jumped in front of me. The spike hit him in his chest. However, he was not hurt and there was no blood. The two zombies jumped on top of Azznic. To me it looked like they were eating him.

"Please… please don't eat him." Judas pulled the spike from his chest and threw it on the ground. There was no trace of where the spike hit him. "Remember the last person you ate?"

The skeletons backed off Azznic who now instead of looking like a metal monster, looked like a giant piece of scrap metal. When I looked at him again, I saw something fall out of him.

"The Aquarius Gem." Judas said walking over to it.

"It's for you, Cyrus." Sofia folded her arms. I walked over to where Judas was standing. "Take it," he said. "It's yours to keep."

I looked at the skeletons sitting in Principal Cole's chair. Then I looked back at Sofia.

"I can't," I said. "I just can't."

Sofia walked up to me and put her hand on my shoulder. "They sent it for you. That is why Mr. Cazzner… Azznic came back."

Judas's red eyes met with mine. "Before you take it, you should take off the bandage. With the Gem, you won't need it."

I had forgotten all about the bandage Garner had given me. "How did the bandage stop the bleeding and make me feel better?"

"Easy," Judas said. "When the dead gives any- thing to the living, it enhances the livings body. Also the dead has enhanced strength and I don't mean the strength of fake heroes. I mean enough strength to rule the universe, and that's just one power."

"Um… cool." I said trying not to look at Gertrude or Garner. "So anyway, this Gem thing, it's for *me*."

"It's all yours," Sofia said smiling at me.

I could not believe Sofia actually smiled. She never smiles unless it is a wicked evil smile. However, this smile was actually heartwarming. That is when I knew I needed to take the Gem. I took off the bandage and handed it to Garner.

"Thank you." I turned around and walked toward the Gem.

"You're welcome lad."

I tensed up as I turned around slowly. "What?"

The other skeleton Gertrude laughed, "Just because we're dead doesn't mean we can't speak, sonny."

I turned toward Judas.

"What?" He asked.

"Nothing," I said. I took a deep breath and picked up the Gem. It glowed in my hand.

"Whoa." It tickled my hand then disappeared. I looked around the room. "Where did it go?"

"On your wrist." Sofia said as if it was obvious. I looked at my wrist and saw a silver watch around it. The Gem was inside the watch glass. It looked awesome.

Judas gave me a gruesome smile. On the other hand, in his eyes, it was a heartwarming smile. "Only you can take off the watch. I would warn you not to take it off though. If these Gems got into the wrong hands like before-"

"The world would be destroyed and end up in chaos again. Only this time it will be for eternity." Sofia said finishing for Judas.

"Wait a minute Judas, where's Collin and Connor?"

Judas sat on the ground. "Well Mr. Cazzner brought us in here and he killed Mr. Cole with metal spikes. Then Collin and Connor tried to run of course, but then Mr. Cazzner did the same thing to them that he did to Mr. Cole. But I didn't see him actually kill Collin, I was unconscious a bit."

I was barely listening to Judas's story because I was too busy looking at my new watch. I never wore a watch before, but I guess I could make an exception this time.

"Cyrus and Judas, we have to get out of here," Sofia said running toward the door. "Let's go!"

"Why?" Judas and I said simultaneously.

Before she could answer, Mr. Daster walked in.

He eyeballed us down. "Where is Mr. Cole? I need to speak to him right..." His green eyes widened as he looked over at Gertrude and Garner still sitting in Mr. Cole's chair laughing and talking.

"Fine, let your new friends sit in that chair. That's not my problem it's-" He stopped again and saw Mr. Cazzner who somehow did not look like that scrap piece of metal anymore. He was back human. "Mr. Cazzner?" Mr. Daster said shocked.

"I'm all right" Mr. Cazzner said getting up from the floor. "Although these children attacked Mr. Cole and sent him through that broken window. And those things you see in that chair are students in disguises. They disguised themselves so we would not know who they are. I came in and saw the whole thing with my own eyes." He looked at Gertrude and Garner. "Pathetic things. You're disgusting."

"'Things'?" Judas was about to attack Mr. Cazzner, but Sofia and I held him back. Judas yelled. "You better be glad they're holding me back!"

"Well I never," Mr. Daster said. "Triple detention for you all. On second thought... expulsion!"

"What?" Sofia yelled.

"Don't count on it." Judas broke free from our grip. "Gertrude, Garner if you would please help with these two, without hurting or eating them."

"Whatever you say, boss." The two stood with smiles. They held Mr. Daster and Mr. Cazzner up against the wall.

"We got to go," Sofia said.

"Where's the book... Azznic?"

"What book?" Cazzner asked with a crooked smile.

"Fine." The silhouette came out of Sofia. It paused then went inside Mr. Cazzner's body. Mr. Cazzner grunted.

"I won't tell!" Then his pupils widened a mile. "The third drawer in my desk, the one with the lock."

The shadow left Cazzner's body and went back inside Sofia. Cazzner's eyes closed then he sighed.

"What in the name of Jacob's ladder is going on here?" Mr. Daster asked. "How was that shadow thing moving? Who is Azznic? Is this some kind of prank?"

Sofia and Judas ignored him and walked out the door. I followed behind and could hear Mr. Daster yelling for help. Before we could even reach the classroom door, the bell rang. All the kids filed out of the classrooms talking loud and fighting, as always.

By that time, we made it in the classroom with a group of kids. They were throwing paper airplanes, giving each other wedges, chewing and popping gum, and doing many other mischief things. We walked up to the desk.

"Cyrus, open the lock," Judas said.

"How?" I asked. "I don't have the key to it."

"We may not have a key, but we do have Aquarius which…" He paused for me to fill in the blanks.

"Controls any and all things that are met-al." I said.

"Right, and you have the Gem, so open the lock."

I was about to try and use the Gem when I noticed Sofia was gone.

"Wait, where's Sofia?"

"Right here," Sofia came in. She threw Judas and me our backpacks. "Everything from your locker is in there."

"How'd you get all of our stuff?" I asked.

"Uh, shadow," she answered. "By the way, open the lock so we can leave."

I nodded. I honestly did not know what to do. I held out my hand toward the lock and it turned to face me. I had one word to say, "Cool."

I closed my hand and the lock broke leaving pieces of metal on the floor. "Sweet!" I then realized that no one was paying attention to us. Not that I was complaining.

"Good." Sofia ran over to the drawer and opened it. "I got it." She pulled out an old torn up leather journal.

"Why do we need a journal again?" I asked.

Judas rolled his eyes. "You'll see O'Hara. Now let's get out of here."

The three of us walked through the hallway out the double doors. We ran to the edge of the property and then we saw him. Collin. He had a knife in his hand and he did not look happy.

"Come here, Judas! Now!" His clothes were torn and his eyes were blood shot red.

I held out my hand toward the knife and it obeyed me. It shot out of his hand and into mine. "I can't believe that worked." I said happily.

Sofia grabbed the knife from me. "Of course it did."

"Don't worry, I got him." From behind Judas came a zombie.

"What is that thing?" Collin pointed to the zombie then fainted and fell to the ground.

Judas pulled his hair. "Would you all stop calling them things!"

"Hey Guys!" Sofia was looking in a small ditch where Collin had fainted.

Collin began to slowly stand up and try to get his balance.

Judas and I ran over to the ditch and looked in. Principal Cole and Connor were lying at the bottom of the ditch.

"They're dead," Judas said. "But they didn't die from Azznic's spikes, or a knife." He rubbed his chin.

"How do you know that?" I asked. "Be-cause, I have the power to know how someone died. They were choked to death and it wasn't Collin or Azznic that did the choking."

"So who was it then?" Sofia said.

We heard a moaning from behind us. Collin was still trying to get his balance when he looked over and saw the skeleton. He fainted again.

"We don't have enough time," Sofia said putting the knife in her sleeve.

"Let's go." She started running off at top speed with Judas trailing behind her.

"Wait up!" I tried to catch up with Judas, but he was going way to fast so I did not worry about it. "Guys wait..."

Sofia and Judas stopped in the middle of the town. "Oh, thanks for waiting," I said catching my breath.

Judas glanced back at me. "We didn't stop for you."

"Look." Sofia pointed ahead at a construction site.

"I told you we should've gone right." Sofia slapped Judas's shoulder.

"Great, now what?" I asked. I had my hands on my knees. I was still catching my breath.

"Cyrus!" Judas put his hands on my shoulders.

"You can take that big piece of metal and float us to the other side." I looked at the giant piece of metal. It will hold the three of us, but there was a problem.

"Wouldn't it be weird for people to see three kids floating on a piece of metal in the air?"

"It doesn't matter!" Sofia pulled my arm and pointed at the metal.

"Do it."

"But it'll be too heavy."

"Do it, Cyrus!" They yelled in unison.

"Okay! Okay!"

I took a deep breath then lifted my hands up. It took four tries to get the metal to respond. After that, my arms moved as if I was playing Tug-of-War. I laid the metal in front of us.

"That was hard."

The three of us stepped on top of it. I gently flew us above the construction site. By gently I mean almost causing us to fall every five seconds. To my amazement, no one noticed us. I looked down and saw a construction worker river dancing while all the other workers clapped for him. I set us down on the other side. I looked back at the man dancing. He was still going; the others still applauding and cheering, with no one noticing us.

"Come on Cyrus," Sofia glimpsed at the workers.

"For the record I had nothing to do with that. Honestly."

Judas was about to walk away, but then he stopped. "Cyrus where's your house?"

"Why?" I asked still looking at the dancing man.

Judas took a deep breath. "Because."

"Because why?" I said walking over to him.

"Enough." Sofia came walking up behind me. "We have to keep moving. Cyrus, lead the way to your house now."

"Alright." We walked all the way to my house. When we got there, I took the key from underneath the doormat and opened the door. We walked inside and saw Peter.

He was sleeping on the couch, as always. The TV was on WWE, popcorn and cheese puffs were spilled everywhere, and a 20oz root beer was half emptied.

I looked at Peter's snoring face.

"Um… bro?"

Sofia rolled her eyes. "Peter O'Hara would you be so kind to awake from your unimportant nap!"

Peter's snoring stopped and he rolled off the chair to the floor. He took off his sunglasses and looked up.

"Cyrus? You're home early. What-" He stared upward and saw Judas,

"What are you doing here?" Then Peter looked at me again and saw the Aquarius watch. "He knows, doesn't he?"

Judas nodded.

"Okay, he knows. We'll leave before sunrise. Everyone go home, get some rest and pack." Judas and Sofia nodded and ran out of the room.

"What?" I honestly had no idea what was going on today. Now, my brother is saying we are leaving. "Where are we going?"

Peter knelt down in front of me and held my hand very firmly. "We leave to find the Temple of Zodia."

I felt a big smile come across my face as I repeated "The Temple of Zodia."

Where We Need to Go

You've probably been on vacation before. Well this will not be a vacation trip. Imagine trying to go somewhere and you don't know how to get there – no map or anything. But either way, you're in your room packing your bags to go to the Temple of Zodia... *wherever* it was. This was our position. While I was packing however, I remembered Mr. Cazzner's... *Azznic's* journal. Maybe that would help us with our journey.

Early the next morning I walked downstairs with my small duffle bag, and I was surprised to find that Sofia and Judas had returned. We had to work fast because it was close to sunrise. Sofia took out the journal and placed it on the table. The four of us sat at the kitchen table staring at the journal.

"Let's see what we have here, shall we." Peter turned the journal toward him and started reading:

In the year 51 B.C.E. I found myself wandering aimlessly through the Sahara Desert. Aquarius abandoned me and now I am forced to dwell alone. I eventually found myself in front of a fortress in Alexandria...

Judas walked to our refrigerator and pulled out an arm full of root beer cans. "Alexandria? As in Alexandria, Egypt?"

He sat down and turned the journal facing him.

…Two guards gave me a fatal warning. I ignored it of course. They knocked me to the ground and said this was my final warning. I got angry. I sadly turned into that creature Azznic. I killed both guards and stormed through the castle… I eventually found the throne room. Ten guards stood in front of an Egyptian queen. It was the lovely young Cleopatra…

"Cleopatra!" Sofia grabbed the book off the table. "The Elders are so stupid! Allowing Azznic to…"

"Sofia!" Peter stood from his chair. "The Elders are omnipotent and omniscient in case you've forgotten! Which I highly doubt you have!"

She sat the book back down on the table. "Whatever." She started reading the book.

…She waved eight of her guards to attack me. I swatted four away and pounded the others into the ground. The remaining two guards quickly moved Cleopatra into another room. I burst through the doors and found myself staring at numerous guards with spears ready. I felt an excruciating pain in my back and sides. Three guards had pierced my

metal skin with their spears. I shall never forget the words Cleopatra spoke to me; "The Elders and myself despise you, Azznic." I awoke here in front of the Strait of Gibraltar back as Carlton Cazzner. I cannot remember what happened after Cleopatra's words. Perhaps the guards dragged me here, or maybe Aquarius and the Elders haven't given up on me. Or perhaps it was all luck.

Judas burped as he finished the rest of the root beer. "So he started in the Sahara Desert, then Alexandria, Egypt and now he's in front of the Strait of Gibraltar. Is there a pattern?"

Sofia pulled out a large map from her pink duffle bag. "Here's Africa. He went from the Sahara to Alexandria then to Gibraltar. So right now he's in between the Strait of Gibraltar and the Atlas Mountains."

I looked down at the map and retraced the places. "Why was he in the Sahara to start with?"

"Ask the Elders, bro." Peter leaned back in his chair.

The name Elders rang a loud bell in my head. Maybe Sofia didn't want me to remember. "Right, who are the Elders again?" I probably should not have asked. They all looked at me as if I was stupid. Not that I cared, I was used to it. Besides, *it* was probably Sofia.

Peter shook his head. "The Elders of Zodia are the keepers of the Zodiac Gems. Like I reminded Sofia, they are omnipotent and sometimes omniscient. They are known by three names; the Elders of Zodia, the Sacred Twelve or the Zodians. They pick out certain people or animals to do their bidding. When they are through using them, they toss them aside. It's sad actually."

It was all coming back to me now. I remembered in stories about how the Elders built the Temple and charmed it so only they could enter.

Sofia looked out the window. "We have only a little while until sunrise. We have to leave now." She put the map and journal in her bag and started for the door.

When she got to the door, something fell out of her sleeve. It was the knife Collin had. It had dry blood on it. The bloodstains were not there before. She picked it up then paused. She looked back at us. "Well, come on."

Judas trailed behind her with an empty root beer can in his hand. I was right behind him until I looked back at Peter. He had a bow and quiver in his hands.

He walked passed me and laughed. "I must have forgotten to tell you that I am a skilled archer." He patted my head. "Alright, let's get a move on."

We walked all the way through town until we reached a small, badly painted wooden sign that read, Now Leaving Callisto.

"Now what?" I asked. "Do we take a bus, train or plane?"

"Nope," Judas pointed at the road up ahead. "We travel on foot for now to avoid danger." I would soon learn that it was safer not to use public transportation right then.

I touched the wooden sign. "Right, now where exactly are we heading?"

Peter smiled at me. "Africa."

Sofia put her hand on my shoulder. "Well, stop standing around. Let's go."

The Zodian god of Intellect

So, the plan was to get from Germany all the way to Africa. Geography was my best subject and the only subject I ever made a B in. Because of this, I thought that I would be able to create a path on the map by myself, right?

WRONG.

Sofia wouldn't even let me *look* at the map. Because she made an A in geography that meant that she got to handle the map. I wanted to vote on it, but the voting never happened. I did not have much of a chance against Sofia anyway.

We stopped to rest, when Sofia came and sat beside me.

She had the map in her hands. "Okay, so we're coming from Berlin, Germany. We will go through Germany then France and Spain, somehow cross the Strait of Gibraltar and Atlas Mountains then the Sahara Desert. If we do not find anything there, then we will make our way to Alexandria, Egypt. How does that sound?"

I tried to think of a better plan, but nothing came to me fast enough. "Well, it's okay I guess."

"Do you have a better idea?"

I didn't want to say no, but I had to. "No."

"Alright then," she said.

"Wait a minute. Why do we have to find the Temple of Zodia? Not that I'm complaining; I'm just wondering."

"Because, Garner and Gertrude can't hold Azznic or Mr. Daster forever. Since Azznic knows we have his journal, he will know where to find us. That'll be his chance to kill us."

I had totally forgotten about Mr. Daster and Azznic. What would Judas tell Garner and Gertrude to do with them? I had to find out. I stood up and went over to Judas who still had the empty root beer can. He was kicking it back and forth with my brother.

I tapped Judas on the shoulder, which gave Peter the perfect chance to kick the can and hit him on the side of the face. The can hit Judas right beside his eye. The strong force of the can caused his head to turn all the way around. Yes, physically his head turned all the way around.

He slowly cracked his head back in place as if nothing happened. "What do you want, O'Hara?"

"What did Gertrude and Garner do with Mr. Daster and Azznic?"

"Don't worry, Garner made sure that Mr. Daster would not remember anything that happened, and Gertrude made sure that Mr. Cazzner was out cold long enough to give us a good head start. After that, they went back to the After Life. Now, if you excuse me, I have to show your brother whose boss with this can."

"You'll have to show him some other time." Sofia stood up and brushed herself off. "We've got to get to France."

I still didn't understand why we couldn't take a bus, train, plane, or any public transportation for that matter. I didn't want to ask, but I couldn't figure it out on my own. "Why can't we take a bus, train or plane?"

Peter pulled out one of his arrows and started to wipe the tip of it with his shirt. "Because, all the Zodiac Gems are named after the Sacred Twelve. They each designed their own Gems and gave the Gems their power. Aquarius made his Gem and picked a mortal to wield it. Of course, that mortal was Mr. Cazzner, whose name was change to Azznic. Aquarius is now mad because Cazzner don't have the Gem anymore. So, if we ride on anything metal there is a good chance he'll kill us. For now, we travel by foot until we know more."

"Oh." I tried not to feel bad considering I was the reason why we had to walk through three countries, cross a straight and desert, then possibly cross another country. "Sofia said the Gem was for me."

Sofia rolled up the map and put it inside her bag. "Gemini and Aries allowed us to attack Azznic because they trust you with the Gem more. They kept Aquarius distracted enough to let you take it."

"Why me, and how do you know that?" I asked.

Judas started to play kick-the-can with Peter again. "Gemini and Aries like you. Sofia and I put in a good word for you. They agreed with us to let you have the Gem. We know this because the creators of the Gems can contact the holder of the Gem; likewise, with the wielder. They only make contact when they want to."

I had more questions to ask, but there wasn't enough time. Sofia walked in front of us and motioned for us to follow.

"Okay guys, we have a lot of ground to cover," Sofia said. "We need to move fast. If we follow my schedule we should make it to France by late tonight."

Peter laughed, "Tonight? Is that possible?"

Sofia looked back over her shoulder. "Yes."

Judas fell to the ground laughing. "We're going to make it to France by tonight? How many breaks do we get?"

Sofia brushed the hair out of her eyes. "None."

"None!" I thought she was insane. "Even if we don't take breaks we still won't be able to make it to France. The distance is too great on foot. It'll be impossible."

"Fine!" She murmured something under her breath and looked at Peter. "Since you're the only adult you take the map." She shoved the map in his hands and walked away.

Peter opened the map. "Okay, so I guess we'll walk for a while and then rest."

"*Really.*" Judas said sarcastically. "That's a great idea."

We have been walking for several hours straight. My legs were burning and I was exhausted. I could not walk anymore.

Peter stopped and stretched. He finally said the words the three of us wanted to here. "Okay, break time."

The three of us collapsed on the ground and moaned. Peter was standing a couple of feet from us and started to practice his archery, he wasn't tired.

Judas grunted as he tried to sit up.

"Sofia, please be in charge, my brother is walking us to death."

She wiped her eyes. "I can't, since Peter is the most responsible, he should…"

"Sofia take the map, please!" I loved my brother but I have to be honest, he wasn't human. It was as if he could not feel pain, he looked refreshed.

"Fine." Sofia went over and talked to Peter.

Judas was lying beside me looking at his root beer can. "How old were you when you first heard about the Temple of Zodia and the Gems, Cyrus?" He asked me.

"I was about ten years old. My dad would tell stories about them to my brother and me for a bedtime story." I hesitated. "When he died, Peter found some books in his study. Our mom didn't really like us reading about the Zodiac gods, so Peter didn't let me read any of those books until I got older."

"I know why. Sofia does too."

I tried to raise my head up but failed. "Why?"

Sofia came walking up to us laughing. "Let's go!"

I got to my knees. "You got the map?"

"No, Peter still has the map, but I get to decide everything else. So, come on."

We walked several more hours and found a small cottage. There was a neon sign on top that said, Kan's Eatery, Burgers, Fries, Hot Dogs, Oatmeal and Pies. Take Outs Available.

Peter licked his lips. "Pie." He took off his quiver and put his bow inside it. Then he put the quiver in his bag. He eyed Sofia.

Sofia walked up to the door. "I guess we can eat now."

We walked through the door to find a guy standing behind a small counter. He had shaggy dirty blonde hair with glowing blue eyes, and he wore a green shirt with a name tag that said Hi, My Name Is Kan. He was talking on a smartphone and spoke like a stereotypical surfer.

"Yeah sis, I'll be home by ten so don't have a tantrum or anything. Don't worry, I'll bring home some food."

He looked over at us. "I gotta go customers. See ya." He set his phone down and smiled. "How may I be of service to you dudes and dudette?"

Peter pushed us out of his way. "I'll take some pie."

Kan pulled out a pen and note pad. "Pie. What about the kiddies?"

Judas leaned on the counter. "I guess I'll take a hot dog."

Kan looked at me and gave me an awkward smile. "What about you little dude?"

"Um... I'll take a burger." There was something about Kan that made me uneasy.

He smiled big at Sofia. "And fries for the dudette."

Sofia's eyes widened. "How did you know?"

Kan laughed nervously. "Lucky guess. Take a seat anywhere, your food will be out soon, amigos."

We sat next to a window that looked like it hadn't been dusted in years. I wiped away some of the dust and looked outside. There was a forest on one side of the building.

I looked at Sofia who had her eyes fixed on Kan cooking. "Are you alright?"

She did not answer.

"Sofia. Sofia. Sofia!"

"Huh! What?"

"Are you okay?"

"Yeah, I'm fine."

"Where's my pie?" Peter looked like he was about to explode.

Judas tensed up. "They have to make the pie first in order for the customer to eat it!"

Peter slammed his fist on the table. "I haven't eaten anything all day! When I don't eat I get angry!" Judas pulled his hair. "It's only like eleven o'clock! We've been walking for like hours now and-"

Thank goodness Kan came. He set our food down and smiled.

"Enjoy, compadres. The meal is on the house."

Peter ate the pie in seconds.

Kan laughed, "Here ya go." Kan set two more pies in front of Peter. "Enjoy." He walked back to the counter.

Peter looked at the pies. "How did he know I wanted two more pies? And how did he know I wanted rhubarb pie?"

Sofia pushed her plate back. "How did he know I wanted French fries?"

Judas looked at his food. "This hot dog has everything I like on it. Ham, bacon, and mozzarella are my favorites. How did he know that?"

I was too scared to see what my burger had on it, but I looked anyway. It had the condiments I liked so I took a bite out of it. It tasted like the burgers my mom would make me when I was younger. "No way."

Peter looked at it. "Mom's burger?"

I nodded my head, yes.

Sofia reached for her food, but snatched back. "Okay, this guy is starting to creep me out. Let's just stop and think for a second shall we. He knew the exact condiments we like on our food. He knew what I wanted to order before I even said it. On top of that, he knew what type of pie Peter likes. So does anybody have any idea what this means?"

Judas shrugged. "He's a good guesser?"

Sofia rolled her eyes. "No, which of all the Elders can read minds and have a sister?"

I looked at Sofia. "Cancer" I said.

Peter looked at his pies. "Of course, Cancer can read minds."

"He can also levitate things, and he's the brother of Gemini." Sofia added.

"Correct." Kan said walking up to our table. "You see out of all the Elders I'm the… most fun. I'm the one that was banished from the Temple."

I read about how Cancer was band from the dwelling place of the Sacred Twelve, but history never said why.

"What did you do?"

Cancer pulled up a chair. "Well you all know about how the original Temple of Zodia was somehow destroyed and all the Gems were scattered everywhere. Well… that was my fault."

"What!" Sofia's eyes started to glow.

"You're an idiot! No wonder they don't want you anymore!"

Cancer sniffled and put his hand over his heart. "I know. Now my sis is the only one that talks to me. At least she still likes me… I think."

Peter stood from his chair. "Well we better get going. See you later, Cancer."

Cancer stood from the chair. "Please call me Kan. That is with a *K* not a *C*. Here, take some food with you before you hit the road."

Judas stood up at the counter. "Do you know where the Temple of Zodia is Kan?"

Kan laughed. "I'm not supposed to know where it is, but I do. But, I'm not allowed to say the Temple's location. There is a sacred vow to keep it a secret for eternity. And since I live for an eternity, I won't say." He handed us our food and walked us outside.

Kan touched Sofia's shoulder and whispered something in her ear. Her eyebrows furrowed, and she walked away.

He grabbed the back of my shirt and grinned. "Here little dude. You'll probably need this." He handed me his smartphone from earlier and walked back inside.

"Cyrus." Peter called in the distance. "Let's get going."

Zodiac Saga 1

My Eternal Secret Uncle

While we walked through the forest, I looked at my new phone. To my surprise, Kan still had all his contacts on the phone. Every Elder's number was in the phone. I was amazed to know that they all had phones. I looked at some other documents. He had Internet access, one million fifty-seven thousand four hundred dollars in his bank account (don't ask me how I know that), and there were a lot more things on the phone.

I honestly only cared about the games. He had an awesome football game and a surfing game. He had a built in special GPS that gave exact directions to the Temple of Zodia. Like Kan said, he couldn't *tell* us where the Temple was. Technically, he wasn't even giving the direction, the phone was.

"Cool phone," Peter said coming up behind me.

"Thanks. I guess Kan wants us to find the Temple of Zodia after all."

"Maybe he wants us to correct what he did wrong? Destroying the Temple and scattering the Gems." Peter insisted.

"Even if we do correct his wrong, we'll get the credit." I told him.

"Maybe he doesn't know that, or maybe he just doesn't want to believe it."

"We still have to find the Temple. Wait, if the Gems are scattered everywhere why are we looking for the Temple?" I asked.

"Because, the Elders of Zodia has a map that shows where all the Gems are located." he told me. "Whoever has the map will get the Gems."

My phone started to beep. I was getting a text from… *Aquarius*? The text read:

Cyrus O'Hara, watch your back fool. That is still my Gem and I want it. I will have it one way or another.

Aquarius

I got scared. I know Aquarius was stronger than the Gem, so anything could happen. I swallowed my fear and kept walking. I didn't even tell Peter what the text said.

We finally made it out of the forest. There was a meadow of flowers that lead to a huge mountain the same color as Judas's hair.

"Wow." Sofia came running up. She took a picture of the mountains with her camera and looked back at us. "Which way do we go now?"

My phone made a grinding noise then the special GPS logo popped up.

"Go over Mt. Ronan. Once there an Elder of Zodia will send you a guide for more assistance," It said.

We listened. We were halfway through the meadows when Sofia pulled me over to her.

"Don't trust her," she said, walking away from me.

I had no idea who she was talking about. "Don't trust who?" There was no response, and I just kept walking.

We walked through the rest of the meadows and went over to the mountains. Judas pulled out some climbing equipment from his bag and handed it to us. He started up the mountain first. I was having problems with my equipment so Peter helped. Then we started up the mountain.

I stopped and saw Sofia flying up on her shadows back. She was lucky, but that's when I remembered I could control metal. I controlled the metal areas of the gear and levitated myself up. I passed Judas.

I was almost up to Sofia when my phone started to beep. I secured myself down on the mountain. I was surprised that I could get a signal on a mountain.

I answered the phone and a deep voice was on the other end. *"This phone will self-destruct in, 10, 9, 8, 7, 6, 5..."*

I was in shock. I threw the phone upward into the air. It exploded with metal falling everywhere.

"What was that!?" Judas asked.

"My phone exploded." I levitated myself up again and kept climbing.

We were climbing for a while and I started feeling nauseous. The last thing I remember was falling down the side of the mountain and Sofia catching me. She took me inside a small cave in the mountain. I was sick with exhaustion. My eyes started too close gradually. The last thing I saw was Sofia jumping from the cave and her silhouette standing beside me looking down and watching my every move. My eyes finally closed and I started to have a dream.

I dreamt I was standing in the middle of a foggy cemetery. I was dressed in black pants, a leather jacket, and dark shoes. I could hear the hoot of an owl in the distance, and a flock of bats flew over my head.

I ducked from the flock of bats and saw a black cat sitting on top of a grave marker. I peered through the fog and read the marker: Here Lies a True Friend...

I could not read the name through the fog but the years were 1844-1998. I ducked from another swarm of bats and saw someone or something moving towards me in the fog.

It wore a black robe and wielded a scythe in its hand. It floated closer toward me and I panicked. I looked at my wrist and saw that the Aquarius watch was gone. I ran for my life. I hid myself behind gravestone after gravestone as it continued to come closer. It passed by me and I did a sigh in relief.

It was the Grimm Reaper. It had to have been the Grimm Reaper. Luckily, I was dreaming. I tried to remind myself that it was all a dream. I also tried to wake myself up in various ways, but it wasn't working. Thinking that the Grimm Reaper was out of sight, I stood. I was walking away when I heard something behind me. I turned and saw things rising up from the dirt, skeletons- zombies- *whatever* you want to call them. Either way, they were all rising around me.

They looked the same as Gertrude and Garner only these were bigger and much more gruesome. I ran from them not looking back once. Through the fog, I could see the Grimm Reaper again but this time something was beside him- Judas. I recognized those red eyes immediately.

He wore a black robe like the Grimm Reaper, but he had a sword in place of the scythe. With skeletons charging behind me, and two people (*entities*? *zombies*?) armed and in front of me, there was only one thing to do.

SCREAM.

I fell on my knees and screamed. The earth beneath me trembled, and I heard bloody yells being yelled all around me. A hand was on my arm and its touch burned like fire.

"Cyrus wake up!"

My eyes shot wide open, and I looked around.

Peter was still shaking my arm. He was covered in bandages and his sunglasses were cracked. "Are you okay?"

I sat up straight and shook my head side to side a couple of times. "Yeah I'm fine. What happened to you?"

Peter licked his lips. "Avalanche, if it weren't for Sofia I wouldn't be here. Forget about all that. Why did you scream? Were you dreaming?"

I didn't want to tell him about my dream, at least not in front of Judas. "I don't know. I just screamed." I didn't like lying to Peter, but I had to lie.

"Well, come around the fire so you can get warm," he told me.

We sat around the fire. We were eating some of the food Kan gave us. I remembered the text Aquarius gave me before my phone exploded; I understood why Aquarius wanted the Gem, but I didn't understand why he would not come and just take it from me. I stared at the watch and tapped the glass but the Gem didn't move.

I knew the Elders had immortality, but I wondered if whoever had the Gem would be immortal. I remembered the years carved on the gravestone in my dream, 1844-1998. My math is pretty bad but I knew the person was about one hundred and fifty years old. Could someone actually live for that many years? I have heard of people dying at one hundred and whatever, but one hundred and fifty, really?

Night came quickly again and someone had to watch the fire. I volunteered myself since I knew I would have problems sleeping. While the others slept, I sat by the fire watching the smoke rise as the fire crackled. I could hear the mountain air whispering and echoing through the cave. I felt more relaxed as the fire warmed my body.

Then I thought about the cemetery dream with Judas and the Grimm Reaper thing. I tried so hard to forget about it, but I just couldn't. I looked over in the dark area of the cave and saw two glowing red eyes. I thought it might have been Judas but I was wrong. He was fast asleep with the others.

I stood up ready to fight. Well, I wasn't *ready* per say, but luckily the eyes disappeared. I calmed down and was about to sit when something came flying from the shadows. A large javelin hit my chest dead on and launched quickly back into the shadows. I fell to the ground and I felt the blood leaving my body. The pain stung like a thousand bee stings.

I was too weak to yell. I tried picking up a rock or stick to throw at one of the others, but it was hopeless,

I was a goner. I could feel myself drifting away. As the glow of the fire faded away my eyes shut and I was gone.

Suddenly my eyes opened and I was surrounded by chaos. Fire was burning everywhere and darkness was all around. I was not sure where I was as I stood to my feet. I felt my chest and the blood was gone, but I still didn't feel well. I looked around to see if anyone was there. I saw a shadow moving in the darkness. If I was alive maybe I would be scared, but in the After Life, I don't think anything can hurt you. I tried to walk around but I fell to the ground.

"It's not fair to be dead is it?" The shadow came out of the darkness. He looked exactly like the thing with the scythe in my dream. "Where are my manners, I am Aries. I am also known as the Zodian god of Death. Welcome to the After Life, Cyrus O'Hara.

I leaned over and looked at him. "Is this place…?"

"Is this place what?"

"Uh." I scratched the back of my head. "You know. The fiery den of-"

"Oh no, not exactly. You haven't made your choice yet. It's your choice. You see there are two different paths in here you can take. Come and I will show you your choices."

We walked down a long, rough, gloomy, and narrow road that could barely hold the both of us.

Aries stopped. "This is the first path."

I looked down the path and saw people chased by wild animals, screaming and running from place to place, people having their hands tied and being tortured, they were burned with fire and other things that are too terrible to look at, so I forced myself not to look any more. Aries put his hand on my shoulder.

"Torment. *Pure* torment." We walked onward to another road that was dim and eventually got brighter. It was a true paradise. The grass and trees were perfectly greened and flowers were full bloomed all around. There was perfect sunlight with golden rays. There were people relaxing, smiling, talking, playing games, eating, and doing so many other wonderful peaceful things.

Aries took off his hood. He had white hair and a short beard to match- on the right side of his face. The left side of his face was nothing more than a human skull. The skull was as black as his robe.

"Paradise or torment." You see, everyone who dies comes here, and I give him or her the same choices.

"Who would pick a life of eternity with pain and suffering?" I was staring at the bony side of his face.

"Your guess is as good as mine. Some feel as though they deserve torment because of the decisions they made when they were living." He put his hood back on. "Which life do you choose?"

I couldn't believe he said that. I *was* actually dead; I wasn't dreaming. I was dead, and no one probably knew yet. I looked over at all the people having fun in the good life. In the midst of it all, I saw my parents having a picnic together. A tear came out the corner of my eye.

Aries set his scythe on the ground. "You could go to them, or you could go back to earth."

"What?" I asked.

"I'll give you three choices."

"Why give me a third choice?"

The right side of his face smiled. "You're my nephew."

My eyes widened. Aries the Ruler of the Dead was my uncle. I will believe a lot of things, but that isn't one of them.

"How? My mom and dad aren't Elders. Wait, are they?"

"No, they are your mortal foster parents. You have three choices. You can go to the place of torment, be with your mortal parents in paradise and never leave, or you could go back to earth."

I started to tear up more. I could spend an eternity with the people who I thought was my parents or I could leave and see my friends again on earth. With blinding tears in my eyes, I took one last glimpse at my foster parents and slowly turned away from them.

"Take me home to earth."

Aries nodded and picked up his scythe. "Hold my scythe and you'll return to earth."

"Wait. Who are my real parents?"

"You'll see, Cyrus. Just remember, people don't always tell the truth."

I took his scythe and felt myself fading, only this time in a good way. "Wait, I saw you in my dream-"

"All questions will be answered soon." I looked at my parents one last time. They saw me and waved, but I did not have enough time to wave back. The image of them was gone as my eyes closed.

Suddenly I opened my eyes and saw the fire in the cave again. Everyone was still asleep and I was wide-awake watching the fire burn.

Our Special Guide

I stayed awake all night trying to think who would want to kill me. I looked around in the cave, but I didn't see anyone or anything strange. I thought about what Aries said, "All questions will be answered soon.'" I wanted to know who my real parents were, and why they would abandon me.

I looked at Judas who was spread out on the ground sucking his thumb sleeping. This was the guy who tried to kill me- in my dream but nonetheless. Maybe my conversation with Aries was a dream. I was confused even more.

I looked down at my shirt. It was torn where the javelin stabbed me. There was no sign of blood, but I knew Peter and the others would wonder what happened to my shirt.

"Is it morning yet?" Sofia sat up wiping her face.

"Um… yeah, its morning. Uh… good morning?" I tried my best not to sound like something serious happened while they were sleeping. I did a banged up job.

"What happened to your shirt?" she asked.

"Well, I uh… I…"

"Hungry!" Peter jumped to his feet and reached in his bag. He pulled out a piece of pie and sat down next to me. "Hey Cyrus, what happened to your shirt?"

"I heard something from outside the cave. When I went to look, I lost my footing and fell. My shirt ripped while I was climbing back up." I lied.

Judas sat up and yawned. "How much farther to the top of the mountain?"

They all looked at me. It was my time to shine. "Well, this mountain is 4,634 meters tall. So all we have to do is figure out how high we are now." I felt accomplished.

Peter pulled out the map. "Right, so… Sofia you figure out all that stuff while I finish eating."

Sofia sat down toward the end of the cave. She opened the map. "Cyrus, come here."

I reluctantly walked over to her. "Yeah?" My heart was beating faster than usual.

"What really happened to your shirt?" She asked with a sly look on her face.

"I told you already. I-"

She studied me up and down. "Tell me the truth."

I tried to think of another lie but it was no use. I told her my dream and about me dying.

"Aries doesn't have a brother or sister. Plus, none of the Zodians have children, and you're probably not a foster child."

"Well that's what he said. Maybe the Elders kept their children a secret, and I know I'm not a foster child. Maybe Aries *was* lying."

She rolled the map up and walked to Peter and Judas. "Like Cyrus said this mountain is 4,634 meters. We have only climbed a little over six hundred meters. I'm pretty sure you guys can do the math."

Judas walked to the opening of the cave. "Let's get going." He started climbing up the mountain without his climbing gear. How were his hands able to grasp into the mountain? I assumed the Aries Gem.

Peter and I tried to hurry while Sofia flew out of the cave riding on her shadow. I used Aquarius to fly up the mountain leaving Peter in the dust. I caught up to Judas who was climbing with bare hands.

"Aren't the rocks cold and hard on your fingers?" I asked him.

"I feel nothing, nothing at all. So how's the Aquarius Gem working for you?"

I looked at the Gem and it glistened in the light. "It's working great. I enjoy having the power of the Gem, even though Aquarius wants to kill me over it."

"Don't take it personally. I'm sure the other Elders would kill you to if you stole their Gem."

"Well, remember you and Sofia put in a good word for me with the Elders."

"Don't add me in conversations without my permission!"

Sofia yelled to us.

"Whatever!" Judas rolled his eyes. "You would think after all these years she would mellow and change."

"What do you mean 'all these years'?"

"Wow, look at the time better get going." He scaled up murmuring something in German. German was the best language I spoke besides English but I couldn't understand what he said.

He said, "Already said to much. She was right… as always."

We continued up the mountain as fast as possible. When we found a small ledge up against the mountain we sat down to relaxed. I had to ask Judas some questions but Sofia wouldn't give me the chance. She kept blocking me from getting next to Judas.

"Sofia can I please go pass you?" I started to get frustrated.

She looked at me and said one word, "No."

I sat back down trying to think of a way to get pass her.

"So how much further have we climbed now?"

Sofia pulled out the map and handed it to Peter.

"Ask Peter." Peter turned the map in every direction possible trying to read it. "Okay, we've climbed about twenty meters."

"Twenty meters!" Judas held out his hands to strangle him.

"What!" Peter yelled back.

Judas rolled his eyes. "You're like what, in your early twenties and you can't even read a map!? Give the map to Sofia, now!"

"Fine!" Peter gently handed the map to Sofia.

"Sofia will handle the map from now on!" Peter stormed to the other side of the ledge.

"Nice work getting the map from Peter." Sofia high fived Judas and patted him on the back. "You are more convincing than I thought."

Judas straightened his back. "Yeah, well you know how great I am."

"Wait." I said. They both looked at me and had grim expressions. "You two planned this, to get the map from Peter?"

Judas grunted. "Yes, Sofia and I planned it. Now shush before your brother hears."

Sofia walked by in front of us. "We move on, now."

So, I didn't tell Peter he was just tricked into giving the map to Sofia. Sofia somehow made two other doppelgangers of her shadow for Peter and Judas. The four of us were now flying up the mountain with accelerated speed. We raced a little and had some fun to pass the time. I finally saw an opportunity to talk to Judas as we were side by side flying.

"Hey Judas I need to talk to you." I said in a low voice.

He looked at me and turned quick. "I know what you want to ask me. Yes, Sofia and I have known each other for a long time. A *really* long time."

"Why would she not want you to tell me that?" I asked softly, making sure Sofia didn't hear.

"Some things can't be told. At least not now. Like Aries told you, all questions will be answered."

"How do you know about what Aries said to me?" I asked louder than I wanted to.

Judas licked his lips and flew faster. "My business O'Hara."

I imagined that Sofia told him, but why would she tell him and not my brother? I flew beside Peter and he lowered his sunglasses and looked over at me.

"What's the problem, bro?"

I looked up at Sofia and Judas who looked to be yelling at each other. "Did Sofia tell you I had a dream about my death?"

Peter laughed. "No. You dreamt your death?"

I told him everything about the dream and the conversation I just had with Judas.

Peter stroked his chin. "Are you sure he said uncle to you? Cancer and Gemini are the only Elders who are brother and sister. Plus, you're not a foster kid. You are my brother."

"I know I'm not a foster kid, so Aries had to be lying."

"Well, I would imagine so."

"So Aries is really lying?"

I asked to make sure. Peter didn't answer and he just kept flying. We were flying for hours and I was getting sick again. This time I wasn't the only one. Judas vomited down toward me. If I didn't move over in time, I would have looked like a colorful rainbow that smelled like eucalyptus and rotten eggs.

"Sorry!" he said wiping his mouth.

"We are almost to the top." Sofia said. "We have already covered 2,000 meters."

"I think we should take a break." Peter suggested.

"I second that motion." I agreed.

We kept flying until we found another ledge but it was very narrow.

"This will have to suffice." Sofia stood on the ledge with her back against the mountain. "No one, I repeat, *no one* can move too much or the ledge will break and possibly cause another avalanche."

The four of us stood on the ledge with our backs against the mountain. No one made any sudden movements, however, if we did fall, we still had the Gems. We were there for about thirty minutes. We would have stayed there longer if Judas didn't start vomiting again. It was all on the ledge and it was spreading fast.

"S-s-sorry!"

Sofia looked as if she made a B on a test. "Let's just keep moving."

The three of us left Judas on the ledge to finish his... you know.

He finally caught up with us and smiled. "I think you all will be happy to know that the sickness is gone, and Mt. Ronan got a few new colors."

"Great," Sofia said.

Peter started to gag. "Can we please talk about something more pleasant? I'm starting to feel..." Boom, he puked twice as much as Judas did.

Judas's face started turning green. "It's coming back!" He started to puke again, and the force of his vomit spewed in Peter face and knocked his sunglasses completely off his face.

Sofia threw Peter down a bottle of water and closed her eyes. "Altitude sickness, the higher we get the more likely we'll all get sick."

I was trying my best to ignore Peter and Judas vomiting. "Is it possible you might have some medicine?"

Her shadow stopped and she started digging in her bag. "I do have one thing, but it's a pill and..."

"...and what? My brother can take pills and so can Judas." I told her.

"Well I only have one pill. In order for it to work, the person has to take the whole pill. So who do we give it to?"

"My brother of course!" Like she had to ask.

"Well this is Judas's third time vomiting.

"Well Peter is my brother in case you have some-how forgotten! Plus-"

"Oh! Since Peter is your brother he gets to-"

"I never said that! He just deserves it more!"

"Cyrus! We are fighting over a stupid pill!"

"Give it here!" I snatched it from her and the pill slipped out of my hands and fell. "No!"

"Cyrus!" Sofia held her hands out as if she was about to strangle me, but something hit her on the head.

"Ow!" The word echoed and a rumbling sound started.

"Avalanche!" Sofia and I flew away from the mountain quickly but Peter and Judas were flying too close to the mountain.

They were about one hundred feet from being buried in snow.

"We have to save them!"

"You mean you have to save your brother!"

"There's no time for this!" I flew in toward my brother who was still busy vomiting. His shadow was covered in vomit and it wasn't happy with him. Somehow, I pulled Peter out of the way. My clothes were covered in puke and I started to feel squeamish.

Then I remembered Judas. "Sofia, Judas…"

"I got him, stupid!" She held out her hand and Judas's silhouette moved away from the avalanche just in time.

"Why didn't you do that for my brother?"

"Your brother is still puking on you." She put Judas back on his silhouette and flew off.

When Peter's sickness passed, my clothes were soggy and smelled like molded bread. His puke was all over me now.

"Hey guys, can we stop for a second and let me change clothes?"

Sofia looked at me and frowned. "We're almost to the top, you can change when we get up there. Now come on, Judas is turning green and I don't want to look like you do."

Peter looked at me sadly. "Sorry, bro for puking all over you."

"It's not a big deal." I lied.

"Let's stop quickly and get you changed shall we?"

Peter and I stopped flying for a few quick minutes and I changed clothes. I felt better in dry clothes with a clean smell. We caught back up with Judas and Sofia. Judas was still on the shadow moaning.

He started to hick-up and said something weird. "Curse not the weak my lord, but praise them by power. Power gives strength… right my lord? Yes… yes of course." He clapped his hands like a toddler and started laughing.

"He can't hear you, Judas." Sofia said rubbing his forehead. "He can't hear you now but he will soon."

Judas grabbed Sofia's hand. "He's watching me now. I can feel his eyes on me, is he pleased?" Sofia put her hand over her mouth. "You can feel him watching you?"

"What's he saying?" I asked.

Peter put his arm around me. "No clue."

Sofia took a deep breath. "Well, see… I am not supposed to tell anyone. I mean the Elders might kill me, but Judas is…"

She didn't have time to finish. The mountain started to shake. I looked up and grabbed Peter's shoulder. "Avalanche?"

He shook his head slowly. "No, a sign. One of the Elders sent the guide to meet us when we reach the top. Not an avalanche but a guide waiting at the top."

I looked over at Judas who was still mumbling on about 'lord'. "Which Elder sent the guide, and who is it?"

Sofia bit her lip but didn't respond.

We continued flying even faster. I had to let Judas ride on my shadow since his shadow refused to carry him. I didn't really know how a shadow could have an attitude and emotions, but I volunteered myself to be nice.

Finally, we made it to the top. The sun was shining right on us.

Judas sat up and frowned. "What happened?"

Sofia's silhouettes went back inside her. "I'll fill you in later. For now, we have to find our guide."

"Your 'guide' is right here." From the left side of the mountain came a girl, about two inches taller than me. She wore pre-ripped blue skinny jeans, with a camouflage shirt. Her hair was tied in a rainbow colored bandana. She had a heavy Russian accent.

"Right this way my strange friends." She pointed down the other side of the mountain. Wooden stairs lead down that side. She laughed. "Please watch your step and ladies first." She trailed down with Sofia following her.

The stairs were slippery and creaked like they were there for a few million years, but we finally made it to the bottom.

Our guide laughed. "Oh! Where are my manners? I am Mercy. The rest of you are?" Peter stepped forward. "I'm Peter. This is Sofia, Judas and my brother, Cyrus."

Mercy looked at my watch. "Aquarius, a powerful Gem. Just make sure it doesn't…" she put her finger over her lips and laughed. "…fall into the wrong hands. Now, of course as you all know I am your guide for possibly the rest of your journey. If you have any questions on or off the subject, please ask."

"Well," I said, "which Elder sent you?" She put her hand over her mouth. "I am not allowed to say. Are there any more questions?"

Sofia folded her arms. "Are you a felon?"

"Sofia!" Judas stepped in front of her. "What my friend is trying to ask is, have you ever been accused of breaking the law before?"

Mercy scoffed. "No. I have never been accused of anything. I am a law abiding trustworthy person."

Sofia sighed. "Well I don't trust you. Let's just get going." Five silhouettes came from her.

Sofia made five silhouettes for us to ride on.

"Oh no." Mercy said. "We're not flying on those things. We walk, take a train, bus or plane. I would suggest a plane."

"Plane it is." Peter said pulling out the map from Sofia's bag as he thought about our safety.

Mercy smiled, giving a sense of safety to Peter. "Don't worry, I already have a plane for us. Come on."

We walked a short distance. Then in front of us was a huge solid gold airplane. On the side of it read, Golden Airline.

Mercy stepped inside. "Come now, dears. It's time for you to meet a special friend of mine."

Sofia rolled her eyes. "Who?"

Mercy smiled. "You'll see."

Memo for Our Journey

I am sure some of you have been in an airplane before. Well if you have, I bet it wasn't like this one. Golden statues literally walked around as our flight attendants. They fed us gourmet sandwiches and grape juice.

"So, is everything on this plane made of gold?" Peter asked. I could tell that in the back of his mind he was thinking about our safety for the journey.

One of the flight attendants smiled. "Yes." They were right, everything was real solid gold, no metal. The chairs (which were cushioned with the softest materials), the utensils, the floor- everything was gold.

Mercy walked up to us. "Everything okay?"

Sofia eyeballed her down. "How did you get all this gold Mercy?"

Mercy shrugged and looked down. "My family is rich. Everything we own is gold. Our house, our entire property, our cars, even our grass and pond. You would expect a person to be happy with a life like this, but I am not. Weird isn't it?"

"Sofia looked disgusted. "Almost as weird as you."

Mercy frowned. "Am I really weird Sofia? Or you just jealous of me?"

Sofia scoffed. "Me jealous of you? Please. Look I know who you are and I don't like you."

Mercy opened her mouth to speak, but one of the flight attendants put their hand on her shoulder.

"Madame, we are approaching our destination in less than thirty minutes. You should get to your seat, now, my lady."

"Thank you," Mercy said.

He put his hand on his chest and bowed. Mercy sat on the row across from us, and the attendant sat next to her. His eyes wouldn't stay off of me and Sofia. He whispered something to her and continued to stare.

Sofia grabbed my arm and ran for the food area. "Okay, listen and listen well, Cyrus. That girl, Mercy, is the daughter of Virgo."

"Virgo?" I remembered reading about Virgo being the Elder of beauty and all that stuff, but a daughter. "That's impossible. You said Elders couldn't have children."

Sofia looked around quickly and focused back on me. "They can, but they must take special care of them, according to the vow they took. Otherwise, the child will be killed. Many of the Elders have children."

"If this is true, who is my father? And what do you have against Mercy?"

"That's a long story, we'll save it for another time. And I can't say whose son you are because it's not worth the trouble to me."

"It is to me."

The flight attendant that was sitting beside Mercy was standing with Judas and my brother. "The flight has ended. You get off. *Now.*"

I looked out the window and we were in a swamp. Snakes, crocodiles and other slimy creepy things crawled all around the plane in the swampy water. The four of us filed out of the plane with Mercy and the attendant behind us.

"Fredrick, may you stay with the plane?" Mercy asked.

"Yes my lady." The attendant stepped back in the plane and shut the door.

The rest of us followed Mercy to an old dilapidated filthy house. It was covered in swamp muck and smelled like mothballs. Mercy knocked on the slimy, creaky mud covered door. A skeleton head was pinned on it with its eyes glowing green.

An elderly woman with a terrible hump in her back answered the door. She wore a simple black garment with a hood half way on her head. Her skin was green, but not like a sickly green. Her breath smelled like death and her voice had a dry hissing crackle sound. "Mercy! So nice to see you again. Need more magic dust?"

"Hello, ma'am." Mercy skin turned the same color as Judas'. "These people need your help. *Magic help.*"

The woman smiled sinisterly. Her yellow eyes looked right at Sofia. "Oh! Come in! Come in!" She escorted us into her home. I had a really bad feeling.

"Guys this place is giving me a bad feeling." I told them.

Judas smiled like the woman did. "I like it."

The swamp woman brought us to a room in the very back of the house. She sat in a rocking chair covered in muddy seaweed. The room was full of magical things; magic books, boxes, and bags. We all sat on the ground around a small dusty half broken table with a multi-colored crystal ball in the center.

The uncanny woman leaned forward in the chair. "I am Witch Greta, the witch of destiny, past, present and future. Mercy brought you all here so I can tell you what will happen on your journey. This will be your destiny. I shall tell you the future of your journey."

She walked over to the bookshelf and pulled out a red book that read, The Future of All (it was appropriately titled) Next, she pulled out a pouch that was purple. She sat back down and poured out the dust from the pouch.

Her voice sounded more sinister than before. "Lords of Darkness bring forth the dark future of these immortals!"

The table shook as if there was an earthquake. A black portal opened and a menacing floating face appeared.

"What do you want, hag?"

The witch bowed to the face. "My lord, they wish to hear the fate of their journey."

The eyes of the menacing face widened. "These fools? Surely you could have called me for a more important fate."

The menacing face turned and eyeballed me down. "You have rage in your heart and you must do what is needed when the time comes." The face turned to Witch Greta. "Very well I will allow you to tell their fate."

He said some magic words or at least I think they were magic words. A burst of energy blasted into Witch Greta.

"Thank you my lord."

The face nodded and in a burst of light and a flash, he was gone. Greta faced us and her body turned red. She placed her hand on the red book. "Immortals you shall travel to a country, one shall become a legend, one shall realize their true self, friends shall be made and lost, one shall fall in the desert, and in the end all will be knights of valor." The witch fell to the ground.

Mercy helped her up. "The future has been foretold for your journey. Now you leave." She gave Greta a hug, walked over to the bookshelf, and took a brown pouch. "Thank you, Witch Greta."

Sofia walked toward the table and took the crystal ball and the small pouch from Mercy saying, "I don't think so, Witch Mercy."

Mercy's face turned red in embarrassment. Sofia gave the crystal ball to Judas and she kept the bag. She looked at Peter and gave him a hug. "Come on, we need to leave here."

Witch Greta laughed. "Afraid they'll know about you?"

Sofia tensed up "Shut up."

We walked back to the plane where Fredrick the flight attendant was standing holding a King Cobra.

"Madame, the plane awaits." The snake hissed and slithered inside the plane.

When we walk in the plane, I remembered the conversation Sofia and I had. I am the son of an Elder, but who? I sat in the back of the plane by myself but Fredrick sat in front of me. I had a bad feeling about him.

"Everything alright?" Fredrick was holding the snake and petting it. "Do you need anything?"

My mind was focused on the snake, but I was able to say, "No, I'm good."

Fredrick laughed. "You're not 'good'. If you were 'good' then you would be sitting up front with your friends."

I didn't really pay attention to him. I was busy thinking about what Witch Greta said, 'Immortals you shall travel to a country, one shall become a legend, one shall realize their true self, friends shall be made and lost, one shall fall in the desert, and in the end all will be knights of valor.' The only part I was actually curious about was the person finding their true self.

"Lancaster." Fredrick shook my arm. "Are you listening?"

I scratched my head. "Lancaster? My name is Cyrus."

Fredrick set the snake on the row across from me. "Right my apologies. We will arrive at our destination shortly." He walked away leaving the snake watching me.

I tried my best to stay awake and watch the snake, but I could not. I fell asleep dreaming again.

I was standing in the middle of a pier and no one was around. I was dressed in the same fashion as my other dream. There were neon signs everywhere. The water was dirty and smelled like old gym socks. I held my nose and walk down the pier. I came to the end and saw a girl. She was wearing a long black dress with a veil on her face. She had a box of tissues in her hand. She was crying.

"Father, please help!" She said. "I need you now! You are my only hope! They are all gone and I am left alone. Help me!" She took a shaky breath and turned toward me. Her tears turn happy when she saw me.

She took off her veil. "You're alive!" She ran over and gave me a hug. "You're alive!"

I could now see her face clearly. "Sofia?"

She smiled and dropped the box of tissues. "Did the others survive?"

I looked around. "What others?"

Her eyes watered. "You don't remember? You remember me but not them?"

"Peter and Judas?" I said giving her a tissue.

She wiped her eyes. "Lancaster, not them. They're dead."

I woke up and jumped out of my chair. The first thing I heard was Mercy's voice over the intercom.

"Attention passengers, attention passengers we are now approaching the French boarder. Please get ready to exit the plane. Thank you."

A Juvenile Convict

We walked off the plane onto an airplane runway. We ran as another plane started taking off. Judas barely made it. Mercy brought us in the airport's terminal area.

"Well, here you go. You are in France, and all you must do is fly to your next location. The tickets have already been paid for." She handed us our tickets. "All you have to do is wait."

"Wait a minute," I said. "Aquarius might-" I was worried about our safety flying on a regular airplane.

"Don't worry about him," she said. "I've got it all under control."

Fredrick put his hand on Mercy's shoulder. He was dressed like a bellboy, but his body was still gold. "My lady, we must leave now. People are staring and pointing at me."

"Right," Mercy responded. "Well, I wish you all good luck." She looked at my watch one more time. "Remember what I told you about your watch, Cyrus."

I nodded and she walked off with Fredrick.

"Okay is it me, or is Mercy kind of, weird?"

Judas laughed. "I like her. Witch Greta isn't that bad either." He froze. "The crystal ball." He pulled it out of his bag.

A faint light came from the crystal ball. The crystal ball light showed an image of a man. He had a physique like Peter, only this man was much bigger. He wore a business suit and was standing in front of a white door.

He knocked and the door fell to the ground with a loud and powerful thud, he was very strong. "Uh… I'll fix that later."

"Of course you will," a voice in the room said. "Come in."

The oversized man sat in a large chair that was fitting for his big size. "Now, why did you do this?" The voice laughed. "It's just business. You see she's alright. She is in our holding cells. She won't be harmed if you pay the right price."

The man stood and stomped his foot. The ground shook like an earthquake. "You monster! Give her to me! Now!"

"Right price." The voice said.

"The bulky man jumped and grabbed the man by the neck. "Give her to me now! Or I will squeeze the life out of you!"

The man was short and geeky. He wore suspenders and a yellow grimy t-shirt. "Oh, and by the way, witnesses are watching." He pointed towards us.

The man dropped the nerd. "Samantha?"

Then suddenly the image in the crystal ball went away.

Sofia gasped. "No, no, no, no!" She hit the crystal ball in an attempt to bring back the images but it was gone. She put her head down in her hands with anger.

Over the intercom, a raspy voiced lady said, "Flights to Madrid, Spain now boarding. Repeat, flights to Madrid, Spain now boarding."

We all boarded the plane and waited, there was a delay in take-off. None of us got to sit next to each other on the plane so we all just sat waiting.

I sat beside a boy that was about my age. He wore shades like my brother Peter and one side of his hair was green, and the other side was blue. His shirt and pants were ripped like someone took a knife and cut them.

He looked over at me nonchalantly. "Hi, I'm Lance. Lance Duncan. You are?"

I smiled at him. "Cyrus O'Hara."

He smiled back at me, which gave me the perfect view of his yellow teeth. "Are you by yourself?"

"No," I responded. "I'm here with my brother and two friends."

He slapped his knee. "Friends, I used to have friends. We used to do a lot of fun things together. Some things we did were right, and others were just wrong. Being in the big house can change you though."

I inched over away from him. "You've been to jail?"

He looked out the window. "Yeah, I have. The cops arrested my friends and me, but I escaped from jail. I had a chance to save my friends, but I didn't. I lived on the streets hustling and running from cops. Every time I see a prisoner, I see myself in that position."

"What did you do?" I asked. He didn't answer, and he couldn't.

One of the flight attendants was walking the aisle as we waited for takeoff. She looked over and saw

Lance and yelled, "It's Lance Duncan! Air Marshals get him!"

"See you later, dude!" Lance stood from his seat, broke the glass out of the window and literally flew out the window of the plane.

"He got away." One of the Air Marshals said. "At least we got his buddy."

"What?" I said. "I'm not his-"

The Marshal grabbed my arm. "Save it for the judge, punk."

I knew I shouldn't have used my Gem, but I did. I used the Aquarius Gem and took the metal bolts out of the chairs and pinned all of the Air Marshals to the wall. Everyone on the plane started running around screaming, calling for help, and praying that it wasn't Armageddon.

"Cyrus!" Peter yelled over all the people. "Come on!"

I ran toward them dodging people and ignoring the looks of the flight attendants. "I had to do it! I didn't mean to pin the Air Marshals to the wall! I didn't mean to use the Gem like that."

"We know" Judas said. He was carrying Sofia on his back.

"Let's go!" We ran off the plane as far away as we could. When we got to a safe distance, we sat down and rested.

I looked over at Sofia. "What happened to Sofia?" Judas smiled.

"Nothing, she just wanted me to carry her."

She got down off his back and stretched. "Well *felon*, what were you thinking!"

I stood to my feet. "I didn't know the boy that sat next to me was a felon! I mean… I did, but after he told me."

"Regardless," Peter said, "we need to get out of here. Spain is still far away. We'll take a bus, it should be safe now, I think. No time to waste."

So we started to walk and I looked back at the plane. I could only imagine the fear in the peoples' hearts seeing me pin the Marshalls to the wall with metal. I felt horrible, but I had to do something. What or who was Lance Duncan? I didn't know.

My Felon Friend Makes a Deal

We finally found a bus stop and sat down on the bench. Sofia was staring at me and Judas was staring at the crystal ball. Peter stood and looked to be in deep thoughts.

I whispered behind Judas to Sofia. "Why are you staring at me?"

She pushed Judas forward and he fell to the ground still staring at the crystal ball. Sofia put her hair in a ponytail. "What do you mean?"

I helped Judas set up against the bench on the ground. "You were staring at me, why?"

She pulled out a brush and started brushing her ponytail hair. "Maybe I wasn't staring at you. Maybe I was just admiring the Aquarius Gem."

"You okay?" I asked.

She put the brush back in her bag. "I hate you! Hate you! I know your listening! I hate you!"

"Quiet down!" Peter shook his head. "The bus is here. Help Judas up off the ground and let's go." Peter ran up onto the bus and put money into the money machine for us.

Judas was still staring deeply at the crystal ball. Sofia and I picked him up from the ground and carried him on the bus.

The elderly bus driver looked at Judas as he continued to stare into the crystal ball. "Kids now a day, always being fascinated by the craziest things. Come on kids I don't have all day."

We walked on the bus and sat in the very back by Peter. He grabbed my arm. "Bro, I need to tell you something really important."

I sat beside him and Sofia set Judas beside me who was now sleeping and drooling. I looked away from Judas to focus on Peter. "Tell me what?" I asked.

Peter folded his arms and looked deep in thought again. "I'm not your bro-brother."

I looked around confused by what he said. "What?"

He looked at Sofia who was paying us no mind. "Aries was right. You are a foster kid. Mom and dad found you in a basket on our doorstep. There was a letter in the basket."

He pulled a piece of paper out of his pocket. It was slightly torn and dirty. "I kept it to show you when you got older." He handed me the letter with shaky hands.

I opened it slowly and carefully so I wouldn't rip it. The letter read:

Take my son and watch over him, for I have lost faith in myself to take care of him. May you please respect my wishes and name him what you please, but one day I will return for him. Be prepared and thank you.

Very carefully I folded the letter and gave it back to Peter. "Who is it from?"

Peter patted my shoulder. "I don't know. If I did, I would tell you. For now, let's just relax and enjoy the rest of the ride."

"Easier said than done for you but not for me."

The bus finally stopped and Peter stood up. "Come on."

Sofia walked off the bus first, and Peter stopped me and handed the letter back to me.

"Keep it." He smiled and got off the bus.

When I got off the bus, I saw that the crystal ball started to glow again. I took the ball from Judas. "Now what?"

The crystal ball showed Mercy sitting in a chair tied up in ropes. Her mouth was duct taped shut, but you could tell she was yelling for help.

A tall slender woman wearing a silk white dress appeared. She flipped her orange red hair. "Now," she said, "You are all tied up. No one can hear you and no one can save you. What are you going to do now?" She ripped the duct tape off Mercy's mouth.

Mercy gasped. "First off, your perfume stinks. Secondly, you are the shallowest, hideous, undeserving-"

"Enough." The woman put the tape back on Mercy's mouth. "The message will be sent. Your brother will come one way or another."

Sofia grabbed the crystal ball from my hands. She said something in German that should never be said. "What kind of person ties someone up... and doesn't invite me? I mean seriously, I would have definitely helped tie up Mercy."

"Sofia." Peter took the crystal ball. "Not now." It was almost as if the image on the ball had paused.

Mercy continued to move around trying to get loose.

"No need" the woman said. She pulled out a brush. "Let's make you pretty. Shall we?"

Another woman came into view. She wore a purple dress that perfectly matched her purple eyes and hair. The women looked very much alike. She held up a gold colored dress. "Pretty right? Don't answer that. Now, let's see if it fits."

The crystal ball started to fade and a powerful stormy breeze pushed all of us backward. The back of Peter's head hit a pole. Sofia bumped into me and sent us both flying into a tree. Judas did a cartwheel and hit a tree.

Sofia tried to stand, but the wind blew her back to the ground. "Cyrus, give me the pouch of dust!" She yelled over the roaring of wind.

"What dust?" I replied. That's when I remembered the magic dust she took from Mercy at the witch house. "Here!" I threw it over to her.

"Thanks!" She poured some dust in her hand and threw it in the air.

The wind stopped slowly. I felt the whisper of the breeze in my ear. I don't know how, but it talked to me. It said, "The world shall bow to you, lord." Then the breeze left.

We all stood slowly.

"What did it say?" Sofia asked getting to her feet. I didn't want to say anything, or deny it.

"It said, 'The world shall bow to you, lord.'"

Sofia took her fist and hit the tree. "Let's find Peter and Judas."

"I got him." Peter said coming walking with Judas in his arms. "We need to tell Cyrus now." "No." Sofia pushed me back.

"Not now, later."

"When later?"

"Guys." I knew I shouldn't have interfered, but I did anyway. "Maybe you should tell me *now*. Just saying. You might regret it if you don't."

"*See.*" Peter said happily, "He has a good point."

Sofia stomped her foot. "I have orders to–"

Peter took off his sunglasses. "Orders?"

Judas jumped out of Peter's arms. "For goodness sake! Listen, one day you will–"

Sofia and Peter jumped on Judas. "No!" They said.

"Wait," Sofia said, "I thought you wanted to tell him Peter?"

"Well," Peter said uncomfortably, "*I* want to tell him."

"Why *you*?" Sofia held out her finger at Peter.

I just stood in the background. "Um… guys? Guys?"

"Come on with me." Judas motioned me to follow him.

"Let's leave them alone?" Judas said.

"Where are we going? How will they know where to find us?" I asked him.

"We're going to take the next bus. They'll figure out where we're going. Trust me."

The two of us walked for a bit until the crystal ball glowed again. We sat under a tree and watched the new image on the ball. We saw Lance sitting on a park bench.

He wore a dirty leather jacket and had on shorts that were about three sizes too big for him. "I'm going to pulverize them." He said to himself. "How dare they! They'll pay. All of them."

"Lance?" I said.

"Who is Lance?" Judas asked. "He is the criminal from the airplane."

"*That's* him?" Judas's eyes widened. "He's like our age."

We continued watching the crystal ball.

"Where is he?" Lance said. "How dare he be late?"

"Hold your horses, boy. I'm here." A man with a familiar voice said.

Both Judas and my eyes widened in surprise. Dressed in a dark purple suit was Mr. Cazzner.

"Cazzner?" Judas said.

"How's that possible?"

"Maybe Aquarius still wants him." He suggested.

Cazzner sat beside Lance. "My dear boy," he began, "I am never late. In fact, I am right on time. Now, Aquarius can and will solve your problem."

Lance stood to his feet. "Give me the Aquarius Gem! Now!"

"Hush." Cazzner said. "I don't have it anymore, but I know who does."

"Who? Tell me who has the Gem! Tell me!"

"Alright, alright. The person name is Cyrus O'Hara. He and his friends are on a journey to find the Temple of Zodia."

Lance sat back down on the bench. "Cyrus O'Hara? I've meet him and talked to him before. He seems like a good guy, but if he refuses to give me the Aquarius Gem, I'll kill him."

"Kill him?" Cazzner raised one eyebrow. "Don't kill *him*; kill his friends. Then he'll suffer more from grief. That's when you bring him to me. He has my journal and I want it back."

"Journal? What kind of guy keeps a journal?"

Mr. Cazzner stood. "Find O'Hara and kill his friends, retrieve my journal, and I will make sure you are praised by the highest." Cazzner held out his hand. "Deal?"

Lance hesitated. "Deal." He shook his hand. "They all will fall."

Cazzner patted his back. "Of course they will."

The image faded and the crystal ball went blank.

I gulped hard. "Great, now we're all going to die."

Judas put the crystal ball back in his bag. "Well, Witch Greta did say, 'One shall fall in the desert of time'; maybe that's me or you."

"Or any one of us." We turned and saw Sofia and Peter standing behind us quietly.

Peter had mud on his clothes. "We would have been here sooner if Sofia hadn't tripped me and made me fall in mud."

Sofia rolled her eyes. "You should have been more observant."

"How long were you guys standing there behind us?" I asked.

Peter brushed himself off. "We saw the part of the vision where Cazzner came up to Lance."

Sofia hummed. "Looks like Witch Greta was right, one of us will die. We need to avoid the desert. Though I feel as though she didn't give us all of the details. We need to be careful, or death will happen." She looked at me. "Death to all of us, but two."

That's when I remembered my dream about the pier. I had totally forgotten. Greta said someone would die in the desert, but she never said anything about death outside the desert.

My dream played through my head. Sofia was crying. Even though it was a dream, her emotions felt real. Why was I dressed in black again? How did Sofia know about my dream? What else does Sofia know that none of us know?

Good questions, but no time to get them answered. We walked to the next bus stop and waited for the bus. No one spoke, just dead silence. We waited for the bus in silence.

Peter Goes to Jail

We boarded the next bus and sat down. No one wanted to sit next to each other, so I was forced to sit by a French boy. He kept talking to me, but I had no idea what he was saying. I just nodded and smiled. I looked down the aisle and saw Sofia sitting beside a hobo, and she looked disgusted. I looked over and saw Judas beside an old woman who was speaking extremely loud to him. Peter sat beside a little boy who was admiring his muscles.

I pulled the letter Peter gave me out of my pocket. "Why did you leave me?" I said to myself. "Why?"

The French boy looked at the letter and yelled to the top of his lungs. "Zodiac! Zodiac!" Then he said something in French.

Everyone jumped from their chairs and began to yell. The boy beside Peter ran off and cried for his mom, and the old woman that was next to Judas was hitting him with her purse. The hobo next to Sofia was fast asleep.

Sofia ran up to the French boy. "How did you know that was Zodiac? How did you know we were with him?"

The boy shrugged his shoulders as if to say he didn't understand, and began to speak French again.

Sofia grabbed him up and held him by his shirt. "I *know* you speak English."

The boy gulped. "Yes, well... you see I... uh..."

"You little..." Sofia dropped him on the ground. Her silhouette came out and hung above the boy.

"Stop!" The boy started to shake with trembles of fear.

The silhouette got closer to the boy.

The boy stared at the people then began to yell. No doubt he was trying to earn their sympathy. When no one would come to his aid, he held out his hand and something glowed- a Gem.

Everyone stopped and stared at the boy and the Gem. "I found it. I found a Zodiac Gem."

Sofia put her shadow back inside her. She swiped the Gem from him.

"This is Cancer's Gem. Where did you get it?"

"I found it under a tree one day. Since then I could hear people's thoughts and levitate things."

Sofia looked around and realized everyone was staring at her now. She threw the Gem to Peter. "Come on. Everyone's staring again." She gave the bus driver a stern look to stop the bus and then walked off the bus.

Judas ran behind her followed by Peter who was looking at the Gem. I turned and looked at the boy. His face was pale and he was crying.

"You okay?" I asked. I helped him up.

"She scared me," he said wiping his nose on his sleeve. "I'm sorry I took the Gem" he said.

"No, no it's okay" I said, "that girl is just mean sometimes. What's your name?"

He looked at everybody. "My name is Wilson, Cyrus."

"How do you know my name?"

"I'm sorry, but the Gem made me read your mind."

"Oh… well-?"

"When I tell you this, I will die, so be prepared. I am the son of Sagittarius." Wilson started to glow gold. Cyrus O'Hara one day-" Wilson faded away leaving something behind.

I picked up the dust covered bottle cap. I looked around and everyone was off the bus and still staring.

"Um… this concludes our magic act. Uh… hope you all enjoyed it." Everyone was stunned and no one moved.

"Cyrus, lets go, it's over." Judas motioned me over. I slipped the bottle cap in my pocket and walked off.

I looked and saw Peter using the Cancer Gem. He was levitating rocks. "This is awesome!"

Sofia was leaning against a tree as she stared into the pond in front of her.

I didn't want to say anything, but I had to. "Sofia, are you alright."

"Yes." She didn't even look at me.

"Are you sure? I mean you scared Wilson. Speaking of him, he-"

"I know!" She covered her mouth. "I know what happened. Wilson is fine. His dad just took him away. If the child of an Elder tells their true identity to a mortal, they must be taken away. This is to help keep the Zodians a secret from the mortals on earth."

"That's why you can't tell me who you really are? Or who my father is?"

She doesn't answer.

"Oh… right. Well what happens to the child?"

"It depends on the parent. Mine for instance, couldn't care less."

"So why don't you tell?"

She started to walk off. "Worry about yourself."

Peter ran over to me. "Cyrus, this is great! Check this out!" He held out his hand and a tree uprooted from the ground. Peter moved it into the lake. "Awesome right?"

"Yeah, great. Guess you don't need your bow and quiver anymore."

"What?" He held out his hand and the bow and quiver fell from the sky. "I'm keeping it! It was a gift. Besides, I don't want to keep the Gem; I just wanna have some fun."

"Just thought since you're the only one without a Gem, you would want to keep it." I told him.

"I don't need a Gem to win a fight."

"I guess you're right, bro... I mean *Peter*." I remembered the letter and him telling me am not his brother. It was somewhat weird talking to him now knowing he is not my brother. "We better get going, right?"

He walked away whistling. "Sure."

We started walking then a lady from the bus pointed to us and started yelling. So we began to run until we found a truck stop.

At least three-dozen eighteen-wheeler trucks were in the parking lot. We went inside to find the drivers to the trucks.

At the counter was a lady about Peter's age. She wore a tidy shirt with pink skinny jeans and a hat that read, I won in truck pulling.

She looked at us. "Hi ya'll! Come on over here! Don't be shy!" Her accent was heavy and strange.

We walked up to her. Now I had a better view. She was muscular and wore too much makeup, which brought out her mustache. Yes, a lady with a mustache.

She smiled and I saw that some of her teeth were missing. "My name is Caroline. Our specials today are bacon breakfast, tater tot surprise, onion ring sizzle, pizza parmesan, chicken stew, and sweet potato pie. What would ya'll like?"

Peter grinned. "I'll take the-"

Suddenly a truck driver pushed Peter over. He scratched his short beard and said "Listen miss, my meal is cold. Why is it cold?"

Caroline frowned. "I'm sorry sir. I didn't..."

He held up his fist. "Fix it now!"

"Hey!" Peter pushed the man back. "First off, you don't push people out of the way, you wait your turn! Second, you don't yell at people, Understand…" Peter looked at the man and then he froze. "Jebediah?"

The man put his hand in his pocket and pulled out a handgun. "Quiet!" He brandished the gun in air as he headed for the door.

The people were hiding and ducking down to the ground calling the cops. I was also ducking, but when the man passed I held out my hand. The gun flew out of his hand and into mine. I caught it and jumped up from the floor. The man looked puzzled then shook his head in rage.

Judas stood and his eyes started to glow. In front of him were two figures that rose up from the ground. It was Gertrude and Garner. Judas pointed towards the truck driver.

Garner laughed. "Yes, sir!"

They ran after the truck driver with us following behind them.

They chased him all around the parking lot until the man finally yelled, "Stop! Just stop." Out of breath, he wiped his face and looked at me. "That gun isn't loaded. It is for show only. Can I have it back?"

I looked at it and pointed it toward the sky. "Give me a second."

"Cyrus, no!" Peter yelled, but it was too late.

I pulled the trigger and it fired. The power of the gun was so strong it blew me backward onto the ground. The bullet went high into the clouds and curved back downward towards us at top speed.

"Run!" Peter jumped behind a trashcan, and the rest of us ran behind an eighteen-wheeler truck. The man just stood there and closed his eyes.

The bullet fell to the ground and exploded like a bomb. The building was scorched, the trucks were destroyed (including the one we hid behind), the entire parking lot was caved in, but the man was still standing with his eyes closed. He wasn't injured.

"Jebediah!" Peter stood from the melted trashcan. "Look what you've done!"

The man laughed. "Me? I did nothing but stand still. The boy pulled the trigger. Everyone here saw who pulled the trigger."

Everyone started to get up from the ground and seemed to be okay. Caroline walked over to us. "We saw everything." She held up a camera and took a picture of me. "Boy, you going to be on the fuss box tonight for this explosion."

I stood up. "The what?"

Sofia pushed me back down. "TV."

"Oh." I looked up and saw Gertrude and Garner in a black truck with red flames and no trailer.

"Come on." Judas ran over to the truck and jumped in. The rest of us followed, except Peter.

I stopped. "Peter, come on."

"No, go on without me." Peter cracked his knuckles.

"Let's finish this Jebediah."

I started to run back for Peter but Sofia grabbed me and pulled me inside the truck.

"Drive." She said. We pulled off leaving Peter behind. I imagined he would be okay, but I took one look back and saw him with his bow and quiver. Then, I was worried.

Garner drove and Gertrude sat beside him upfront. Judas squatted in between the two of them. Sofia and I sat on the bunk beds in the back. I was still thinking about Peter. I hope he don't do anything like what

I just did. I cannot understand how a small handgun can cause so much damage.

There was a small TV in the dash compartment of the truck. Sofia took the remote and turned it on. She surfed through until she found a news channel.

The French news reporter started to speak, (in English). "Breaking news, a local truck stop was destroyed by a delinquent. Witnesses say a boy unleashed a bomb and scorched everything. Here is one of the witnesses."

They showed Caroline. "Yeah, the boy's name is Cyrus O'Hara. He tried to frame an innocent man for what he did. There were others with him, but he was the leader. Again, his name is Cyrus O'Hara and this is his picture." She held up the picture she took of me. I looked pretty good.

"Ya'll better watch out for him because he is dangerous. If you see him, call for emergency help. He should be in jail with this guy they left behind. You hear that Cyrus? You are going-"

Sofia clicked off the TV. "Well, we know where they will send Peter."

Judas sighed. "Garner, find the nearest prison. And you know the one I'm talking about."

Garner tapped the steering wheel. "Gertrude dear, radio please."

Gertrude turned on the radio. It was playing a song by Mange-Keen. Gertrude laughed. "Songs these days."

After a long ride we pulled into a prison parking lot. We parked and jumped out and ran to the door of the building. Judas began to bang on the door. It looked nothing like the prisons they show on TV.

This one reminded me of the After Life. The building was red and looked like it was on fire. The whole building was covered in barbwire. Blinding lights shined everywhere.

Men with guns were lined up around the top of the building. Except they weren't men, they were monsters. All of them simultaneously jumped from the roof, and landed on their feet- or hooves- or talons- or *whatever*.

I heard footsteps coming towards the entrance. The door was bulky and very unusual like a dungeon door. Out came a man dressed in a black jump suit with brown boots and a hat to match. He wore gold medals and a bronze medallion. The one thing that caught my eye was his eye. He wore an eye patch over his right eye. The other eye was pure black.

His accent told us of his Russian decent. "What do you want?" He looked out at the truck and saw Gertrude and Garner, but did not seem to be concerned about them.

I walked forward inside the door. "We're here to visit Peter O'Hara."

The man put his hand on one of the monster's shoulder. "Welcome to Scorpio Sauna Prison. I am Edward von Tomb. Follow me."

All the monster men jumped back up on the roof.

Inside the prison was tormenting and scary. The walls were brimstone and burning with fire. The floors were covered in spikes. Spirits flew everywhere and spoke death chants to us. The cells were oozing slime, and the metal bars were burning flames of fiery metal. Inside every cell was a monster.

Edward Von Tomb stopped. "This prison was made by the Zodian Scorpio to lock away any monsters that caused trouble in this galaxy. Some monsters pledge their loyalty to me and became guards and prison workers. Others stay in the cells. Criminal humans who know the Zodians exist are also kept here. "

"Where's Peter?" I said in frustration.

Von Tomb rubbed his chin. "This area is for the monsters. Follow me to the human area."

He took us to the human section. "Be careful," he said, "Some are *immortal* humans."

"How do you get the human criminals?" Sofia asked.

"When the police take the mortals and immortals to jail, we come and get the most dangerous ones and bring them here. This is easily done because we erase the human memories to protect our prison existence."

He pointed to the cell and pulled out a remote from his pocket. He hit a couple of buttons on the remote. "He is cell 1573. Go ahead."

We ran over to the cell to find Peter lying on a small bed reading a book. He was wearing a red jumpsuit with orange sunglasses covering his eyes. He laughed. "This book cracks me up."

"Peter!" I yelled.

"What?" He jumped up. "Cyrus? Cyrus! Thank goodness, you are here! You gotta get me outta here."

Edward Von Tomb walked up. "No one or nothing gets out of here. Unless someone takes his place."

Without thinking or hesitation, I used the Aquarius Gem to make the cell bars hold von Tomb. "Let's go."

No one followed.

"Come on! What are you waiting for!?"

Suddenly Gertrude and Garner popped up. They started to laugh.

"What's so funny?"

My eyes felt as if they were on fire. "Huh!? What's funny!?"

Garner backed up. "Witch Greta prediction about one who will see their true self" said Garner.

Then I remembered what she said. One of us would see our true self and that one was me. I didn't hesitate to use the Gem. My question was answered. I took the bars off Von Tomb. "Sorry Mr. von Tomb."

He brushed himself off. "Get out and take your friends with you!"

As we walked away, Von Tomb stopped me and the others went on out to the truck and waited. I knew it couldn't be this easy to leave.

He handed me a phone like Kan gave me. "Tell my daughter her father said hello, Lancaster. Her loving father." In the blink of an eye he began to change his form. His mouth opened and his tongue was like a snake tongue. His face melted and he grew yellow scales all over his body.

I ran as fast as I could to the parking lot, screaming. I looked behind me and Von Tomb was slithering on his stomach and hissing. I kept running and yelled, "Start the truck! Start the truck!"

"Okay, okay, I'm on it." Judas hopped in the drivers' seat and drove off without me.

"Judas!" I yelled. "Wait for me! Wait for me! You are not even old enough to drive! Wait!"

I was forced to run and run and run, refusing to look back at von Tomb. He was getting closer to me, so I sped up even more. I was running with all my strength. I finally caught up to the truck when it slowed to get on the interstate.

"Why'd you leave me?"

Judas laughed. "You looked like you needed some cardio. Besides that snaky thing was coming!"

I was in the After Life, and once more I was dressed in dark clothes. I heard footsteps and a man appeared calmly to me. I knew this man was Lance. He looked years older, but I couldn't forget or mistake his face.

His hair was long and blonde with a gray streak in the center. He wore a green toga with a huge flowing blue cape. In his hand was a black scepter with a skull and cross bones on the tip. In his other hand was a scroll.

He held up the scroll and read it aloud. His voice was ominous. "In the distant future, the murder you commit shall lead to your death. On that day you will show no mercy or grace, for you shall follow your father. The sky will turn black and the sun shall fall as the moon shatters. Your friends and loved ones will fear you. In the end, everything in this universe shall bow to you, my lord."

He rolled up the scroll as he fell to his knees and bowed down. His scepter left his hand and flew up into the sky. "It shall be." In a flash, he was gone.

I looked around. "Lance? Where did you go? Is this a joke?" I looked down and saw the scroll on the ground. I picked it up, and it felt as if power went through my veins. The scepter reappeared from the sky and dropped down into my hands.

As I looked at it, the scepter fell from my hands and turned into a metal staff. It stood upright before me as if to say, "I will not bow, you fool."

I woke up startled from the dream. My body was covered in goose bumps. It got worse when I looked on the floor and saw the staff. It was still metal, but the skull and cross bones were wooden. I picked up the staff and looked it over. The scroll was pinned to the staff. I opened the scroll and it was the exact words of Lance in the dream.

I could see a car light coming close and shining through the truck window. I put the scroll and scepter under the cover. I slowly looked out the passenger truck window and saw a car.

A girl got out the car and walked up to the truck. Her eyes looked into my eyes through the truck window. As she leaned in closer peering through the window, she smiled at me. I was somehow able to sneak pass Judas, Sofia and Peter without waking them and get out the truck.

I walked over to the girl, and it was Mercy. She smiled. She was driving a pink sports car. "Do you know how to fix cars?" I could see her bright white smile. "Well?"

I scratched the back of my head. "I guess." I looked under the hood. I started telling her about the crystal ball vision. "The crystal ball showed you in a chair tied up with rope."

She laughed. "What?"

I told her about the image of her and the two women in the crystal ball. After having her stare at me for several moments, I told her about Edward Von Tomb, Snaky Edward Von Tomb.

Her eyes widened when I talked about Mr. von Tomb. "Daddy?"

I reached in my pocket and handed her the phone he gave me. She took the phone and frowned.

She hugged me. "Thank you. Let's go."

"I thought your car broke down."

"Cyrus you need to come with me. I can answer all the questions you want answered. Are you coming?"

I thought about it. Mercy gave me a bad feeling, but I went with her anyway. Inside the car was very strange to me and didn't look like the average car inside.

Everything was pink. The seats were pink leather and it had a racecar steering wheel. In the back seat was a green cat that was staring at me. I looked at Mercy. "I thought everything you had was gold?" She laughed and drove off like a maniac. I didn't even get to look back at the truck. I hoped they don't worry about me too much.

Mercy had the radio turned up loud. There was a heavy metal rock song playing, I could not understand the music at all. Her cat was now sleeping, which totally surprised me because of all that was happening. But the cat wasn't the important thing. Mercy was driving too fast for comfort.

She looked over at me and turned the radio down. "Now, what questions do you want answered?"

I took a good look at her. Her hair was scarlet red. She wore lime green pants and a black shirt that read, Talk To You? Never.

I looked back at her cat again. It was awake and staring at me again. "My first question is: can you slow down?"

She scoffed. "Do you have any questions related to the Zodians?"

"Yes. I have a lot of questions!" Finally, I could get answers. "Who am I the son of?"

She shook her head. "I can't tell you *that*, but I can tell you that they love you very much."

"Do they really? Is that why they abandoned me?" I asked with slight anger.

I didn't expect her to respond.

I moved on. "What does Sofia have against you and your mother?"

She slowed all the way down as if the question brought her guard down. She began to speed back up as she speaks. "Sofia's earthly mother killed my sister, so my mom killed Sofia's mother for revenge. Since then Sofia has hated me, my mother, and everyone in our family. She said she would never forgive us. Oh, and I'm a witch in case you somehow weren't aware already."

I thought about Sofia and felt bad for her. Then I thought about Mercy. "You're a witch?"

She held up her hand and waved it around. "Look at the sky." I looked out and saw the stars. They spelled out: CYRUS O'HARA HERO OF THE ELDERS.

"Whoa that's amazing."

She nodded. "Thank you."

"Why does everyone keep calling me Lancaster?"

"Because that's your real name. There's really no other explanation when you think about it."

"Good point. Does everyone know who I'm the son of?"

She sighed. "We're here." She parked at a hotel. "Here." She handed me money.

"What about the others?"

"Don't worry about them."

It was a tall tan building with tons of windows. It was a five-star hotel but looked more like a six-star hotel. Mercy got into a handicap park, which ticked off an old woman driving an old beaten up minivan. Mercy clapped her hands and I was instantly wearing a brown jacket with a black hood. The jacket had fur on the inside.

She smiled. She handed me a silver whistle. "If you need *anything*, use this. Enjoy, *Lancaster*."

"Wait-"

She pushed me out the car. I put my hood on and shut the door. I waved goodbye as she sped off. Her cat looked out the window, and stuck its tongue out at me.

I stood there with a raised eyebrow at that image. I assumed that was how witch's cats were.

I walked in the hotel. The lobby was empty, but grand. The furniture was amazing. The place smelled like cinnamon and the floors were marble. It was better than Calibri Prep, for sure. I walked to the front desk. The man at the desk had a biker handle bar shaped mustache.

He rolled his eyes. "How may I help you sir?"

His accent was a heavy French sound. I leaned on the desk. "One room please, I would like it on the top floor."

The man looked at me then laughed. "$1,245 dollars please"

I gave a fake smile. "Of course." I pulled out the money Mercy gave me. I had more than I thought. I handed him the exact amount. "Here you go $1,245."

The guy's mouth dropped open. "Th-thank you sir." His hand shook when he handed me my room key. "Your room number is 415. Just ring for room service if you need anything. Enjoy."

I nodded and jogged to the elevator. I hit the button and went up to the top floor. When the elevator stopped, I walked out and went to my room. There was still no one there. I opened the door and everything was spectacular.

A full size kitchen, a bathroom with a hot tub, one humongous round bed, and a window with a breath taking view. I went through the fridge and took out a pizza box and a 20oz root beer and laid on the bed. It was soft and smelled like strawberries. I ate all the pizza and drank the root beer.

As I relaxed more, I finally remembered the others. I reached in my pocket for the phone. That's when I remembered I gave the phone to Mercy. There was no other way I could contact them. I was going to use the hotel phone, but I fell asleep dreaming, again.

I was standing in the middle of a cave with a lantern in my hand. I walked down the cave to a torch lit room. The room was like an office. A desk sat against the left wall with paper thrown everywhere. There is a computer and monitor with smoke coming out of it sitting on the desk. On the right wall, there was a bedroom. Posters of animals, a bed that had bats flying out of it, clothes thrown around the bed that only the abominable snowman could wear.

I heard footsteps and a voice coming from behind me saying "Yeah, yeah I get it. Don't worry I'll find that stuff before they do. I gotta go. See you later."

I hid under the bed. Rats were crawling around under the bed. A shadow walked up to the bed. "Stupid rats. Get away!" I heard a noise like someone was cutting something. "That'll teach you."

One of the rats crawled from under the bed and started squeaking. The *thing* stomped their foot.

It yelled "What? You mean!"

Then the thing picked up the bed and threw it to the other side of the room. That's when I realized it really *wasn't* a person (nothing ever was). It was a gorilla. I correct myself; it was a *talking* and *competent* gorilla that growled at me.

"You, insect!" it said.

Suddenly I woke up in a cold sweat. When I turned my head, I saw something standing beside the bed. I huddled in the corner of the bed.

"What are you?" Then I realized what it was. It was another skeleton. It was dressed in a camouflage uniform.

It smiled. "Master Judas wants to know why you left him and the others."

I got to my feet. "Well, you see I… uh."

The skeleton sighed. "Sometime today please, my master is waiting for an answer."

I walked over to the window and looked out. It was morning. I had a restless night with the dreams again.

The army skeleton put his bony hand on my shoulder. "What answer am I to give Master Judas?"

I walked away and started packing my things. "Tell them I'll be waiting for them here in the parking lot of this hotel."

He nodded, turned into dust, and floated away into the air. I did as I told the skeleton. I waited in the hotel several hours. Then came outside and sat on a parking bump waiting for the others. After hours of waiting they arrived at the hotel.

Peter got out first and ran over to me. "Cyrus!" He gave me a bear hug.

"Why did you leave?" Sofia came out next.

"I went for a walk." I lied.

Judas wasn't buying my lie. "How did you pay for this hotel?"

"I found some money."

Sofia scoffed. "Where did you get the jacket?" Sofia scoffed again. "Well while you were enjoying a luxurious bed, we were sleeping in the eighteen wheeler truck, listening to cars zoom by and blowing horns all night."

I gulped. "Sorry?" By that time, I didn't want to lie anymore. I was more focused on my dream than anything else. "Can we just leave now, please?"

Judas shrugged his shoulders. "Sure, I'll drive."

"No you won't. You don't have a license yet remember." Peter smiled as he got in the driver seat.

Sofia grabbed my arm, and gave me the 'I know you're lying, and I'll find out the truth anyway' look. I snatched my arm away from her and got inside the truck. I sat in the passenger seat to avoid Sofia and her looks. Peter drove off. It was good to have a driver that actually drove the speed limit.

We drove around for a while until Sofia spoke. "We should stop at the nearest mall and buy some clothes, after losing them to the fire last night." She said.

Peter and Judas nodded their heads in agreement.

I looked back at Sofia and Judas. "What fire?"

Peter frowned. "It was a random fire."

Sofia shook her head. "If you were here, you would've known that."

"A random fire started *inside* the truck?" I asked to make sure.

Peter nodded. "It only burned our essentials."

Sofia hummed. "I suggested it was *magic*." I knew she directed her comment at me for a reason.

I ignored her for the time being. My dream was all I needed to be concerned with. I just needed to think about the random talking gorilla that was going to kill me like everything else in my dreams lately. Think about death, *not* Sofia. Death. Not Sofia. Death. Not Sofia. Lance. Not Sofia. Death. Not Sofi- *Lance*! I forgot about my dream with Lance and the scroll and scepter!

"Sofia, can I ask you something?"

She looked at me with pity. "I know you were with Mercy last night, and I know about both your dreams."

I sighed. "How?"

She motioned for me to come sit next to her on the bunk bed. "My silhouette can go *anywhere*."

"So what Lance said in the dream, will it really happen?" I made sure Peter couldn't hear us.

"The gorilla was a person." She said.

I kept the conversation going. "Who was it?"

"The Zodian god Leo's son. He has his father's Gem. The Gem can turn him into any animal, and he can gain their attributes and strengths."

I threw my hands up. "I thought you couldn't talk about the Zodians children-"

She kept talking and ignored the question about the Zodian children. "No one knows what Leo really looks like." "No one knows his original form, including his family or any of the other Zodians. He has always been in the form of an animal or some mixture of different animals together."

I just had to say something about my other dream. "The scroll, is it true?"

She pulled the scroll and rod from under the cover and handed it to me but she did not answer my question.

In an accusing voice she said "Mercy started the fire. In case you wanted to know."

"I imagined so."

"She is honestly the most-"

"Sofia, I know why you don't like her." I was cut off.

"We're at the mall now." Peter parked the truck. "Let's go."

I placed the scroll on top of the rod, and the scroll melted into the scepter. Of course something else supernatural had to happen.

We looked at the name of the mall. It was in French. I walked in and was amazed. France was great. The mall was much larger on the inside, than the outside showed. Boutiques and several merchants were all over the place. Everything was great, until I saw him.

Mr. Cazzner sitting on a bench in the mall. His chartreuse suit almost distracted you from his newly dyed purple hair. He stared straight at me and clapped his hands. He pointed at the Aquarius watch and just walked away.

I didn't chase him. I knew that he wanted me to go after him. A cat and mouse game was not going to be played. My priorities were clothes, not him. My priorities would never be him. I looked around and everyone else was still off shopping. So I picked out four different outfits and went to the register. French people have the most unusual clothes.

I entered another store, but I felt uneasy on the inside. I *knew* Cazzner was still nearby. I bought a few pieces of clothes and payed the rude cashier. Carefully looking before turning my head to leave I saw him again. I nearly dropped my bags.

"Cazzner."

He laughed. "In my opinion, the Aquarius Gem looks better on *my* wrist. You can give it to me now, and I'll tell Lance a half-handed story about how you lost it. He'll believe me. He's not much different than you when it comes to believing lies."

"I'm not playing your games. I don't-"

"By the way, I heard that Peter isn't your brother. Do you know what else I've heard? I've heard that your whole life is a lie. Perhaps death can save you from these falsehoods your friends have and will tell you."

I hate to admit it, but he was right. My whole life was a lie, but I wasn't going to allow him to tell me to die. Something came over me. I balled my fist and punched Cazzner in the nose. His glasses broke when he fell to the ground. I used the Aquarius Gem to put a merchant stand on top of Cazzner to crush him.

I squatted down and looked at the squished and now colorful man. Blood ran down the side of his face. I laughed. "Leave me and my friends alone, or else your pain will be worse." A crowd of people started calling the police. I didn't feel bad or upset, I felt fine. In fact, I wanted to crush Cazzner more. He accepted my violence with laughter. He loved it. But *I* loved it more. I held my hand out toward Cazzner using Aquarius to squeeze the table down on him more, as he wheezed.

"Please don't." More and more blood oozed from his mouth.

"Cyrus stop" yelled Peter, as he Judas and Sofia made their way through the crowd. "Come on stupid head!"

I walked to my friends as if nothing happened. They didn't look at me with fear, it was more like disappointment. The feeling was neutral. They were my friends, but liars. This was going to be a longer trip then I thought. We walked toward the exit, and I walked in the back on my own.

My foot was about to step across the mall exit, but something caught my leg. A loud laugh bellowed from beneath me. "I got you!"

It wasn't Cazzner's voice. When I went to turn my head, I was slammed in the back and brought to the ground. My forehead hit the floor, and I was being dragged backwards by my leg.

"No!" I heard Sofia yell.

Then, everything went black.

The Tormented Zodian

I opened my eyes to find myself lying on a table in a huge library. I could hear the fireplace crackling in the corner. I sat up on the table.

Books surrounded me, each one more colorful than the last. More books rested on what looked to be wooden mahogany bookshelves around the room. A flat pink computer was on the end of the table.

A large black book in the bunch caught my attention: Dark Power: The Beast of Force. It couldn't have been a coincidence that particular book was sitting the closest to me. I picked up the book and opened it.

The first words were highlighted in yellow: 'The beast of force still lives today and forever.'

"How did you get here!?" A voice said behind me.

I dropped the book in shock and turned my head slowly. I staring into the eyes of a… I didn't even understand what it could've been. The thing from the waist up was a baboon, but from the waist down it was a squid.

I slowly stood up and began to back away from it. I was dreaming again. I had to be dreaming again. "What are you?"

It growled and looked directly at me as I continue to slowly back away. "I am Leo, the Zodian god of animals."

"*Oh.*" I scanned him up and down. "That makes sense."

"How did you get here?"

I made it around the end of the table and kept moving away slowly. "I don't know. The last thing I remember is…" What was the last thing I remembered? "Something was dragging me and-"

Leo's head turned into a lion's head, and he roared with the sound of thunder.

"Abigail! Get in here, now!"

There was an awkward silence. During this silence, Leo and I had a staring contest that I was losing badly. The double doors creaked open not a moment too soon, and a girl came into my sights.

Her brown curly hair dropped to the bottom of her back. Her orange dress shimmered with blue sparkles. She reminded me of a nicer version of Sofia.

"Daddy? Is everything-" She looked at me and nodded to herself.

Leo's tone went softer. "Sweetie, who is this?"

She played with the bottom of her dress. "Calvin got him. He said this boy broke into his home." She shrugged.

"Calvin?" Then I remembered what Sofia said. "Calvin is your son, right? He... wait, I never went to your son's home."

Now, from the waist up Leo was a cheetah. "Out!"

I shook my head. "I dreamt I was inside of his cave. Wait... he actually lives in a cave? Isn't that a bit... stereotypical?"

"OUT!" His legs turned into kangaroo legs, and he jumped over the elongated table. With his cheetah claws he cut the side of my face, and I yelled and fell to the ground. He turned to a gorilla, I was thrown across his shoulder. He began to run towards the fireplace.

"Wait! Wait! Where are you taking me!? I told you I didn't-"

He dangled me in front of the fireplace. He smiled in anger. "Stay away from us!" and threw me into the fire.

I didn't feel any burning; I didn't feel anything except a falling sensation. My eyes opened and I was in darkness. I was slowly falling down into nothingness, and I was confused and freezing. Stars began to appear, and for a moment I thought I was falling from the sky. I felt like a falling star in that moment. The wind in my ear whistled louder and louder, and I realized I was falling faster. I was falling *much* faster.

I closed my eyes and braced for impact. I hit the ground... or *something*.

When I opened my eyes, I was... on a plane or in the truck? I was confused and dazed. I looked and saw Peter who was looking out of the window.

"Um..."

Peter jumped and looked at me. "When did you get here and how...?"

I suddenly felt my throat burning. "Throat hurts."

Peter squinted his eyes looking at me. "What happened to your face?"

I rubbed my face from side to side and felt the cut from Leo. "I don't know." I lied… again.

Peter sighed. "Who took you at the mall?"

I cleared my throat as an attempt to soothe it. "Leo's son named Calvin took me."

"Get some sleep. We'll be in Spain soon so get some rest for now." That ended the conversation.

I fought my sleep for hours trying to get Leo out of my mind. I kept thinking about the dream. I dreamed a dream that wasn't a dream. How did I sleep-walk into a random cave that just so happened to be the home of Leo's son? I guessed that someone could've taken me there but what are the odds? At last, I did as everyone else around me was doing. I fell asleep; however, I didn't dream for the first time in days. Thank the Zodians.

I woke up smelling chicken Alfredo. I was laying on a smooth, silky bed. Judas sat on the bed next to me. He handed me a plate with the Alfredo. "Welcome to Madrid, Spain. City most famous for matador fights. How'd you sleep?"

I took a bite of the Alfredo. "I slept pretty good. How long was I asleep?"

He looked down. "A week."

"A week! How?"

"I would lie and say the pill was a sleeping pill, but I don't really lie. So basically, Sofia injected you with a sleeping needle. Just don't talk about it. Okay?"

"Okay. Where are Sofia and Peter now?" I asked setting down the plate.

"They went out. They'll be back…"

"We're back." Peter walked in. "Oh, hey Cyrus."

Sofia rolled her eyes. "I thought the injection would last longer."

"Well it didn't." "What did you guys do while I was sleeping for a week?"

"Nothing." Peter said. I could tell he was lying.

Sofia held up a flyer in front of Judas and me. "What do you think?"

I squinted. "It's in… Spanish…"

She shook her head. "It says," 'Come and watch the most epic matador fight of the century. The matador: Kan Zod. The bull: Renaldo the Strongest and Deadliest Bull Alive. Be there.'

I frowned. "Kan? Does it mean the Zodian god Cancer? Since when is he a famed matador in Spain?"

"We should go." Judas suggested. "It'll be entertaining and help take our minds off of everything."

"Sounds good to me. We should go and keep an eye on him, he's rebellious you know." Peter seconded.

Sofia threw a bag at me. "Okay, shower and change."

We walked down stairs (no elevator), to the front of the building. It had at least twenty windows going up. It was an old looking building. We started our walk to the coliseum. The streets were crowded and everyone was talking around us. There were long lines of people who were obviously excited about Cancer's bull-fight. We got front row seats and settled in.

A few moments later, a man inside a fancy box stood from an oval shape chair. He got the microphone and started speaking Spanish. Sofia translated for us.

"Most honored guests, today we will witness a great fight between Renaldo the strongest and deadliest bull alive and Kan Zod."

A man walked out into the center of the arena, wearing a solid blue matador costume with a red cape in his hand. It was Kan. He laughed and yelled. "Bring on the bull! Bring on the bull!"

A scrawny man walked out of a side door. He was trying his best to hold the biggest bull I have ever seen, back behind the door. The bull was silk black with several horns on his head about 5 feet long, and the bull was at least thirty feet long.

Kan taunted at the bull and yelled "Let him go!"

The crowd erupted into applause screaming "Let him go!" With great force and anger the bull burst out the door and flung the weak scrawny man into the stands. The man landed on three people.

Kan gave the man two thumbs up. "Nice landing!" He looked at the bull and held up the red cape. "What were those words again? Oh yeah. Toro! Toro!"

The bull snorted and charged forward toward Kan. The bull was about three inches from the cape when Kan's eyes made a faint glow. The bull went through the cape and slid into a wall. The wall crumbled.

Kan laughed. "Ole'!"

The crowd repeated, "Ole'!"

Kan faced the bull. "Toro, Toro!"

The bull pulled himself from the wall and snorted. It charged again. Kan looked up at the stands and saw us. He waved. The bull rammed into him when he was looking up at us, and he fell to the ground. He wasn't bleeding.

Kan stood quickly and held his side. "Oh, come on you stupid bull!" He dropped the cape and held out his hand toward the bull. The bull floated into the air still trying to charge. The people became afraid and started to run. They tried to run out of the arena but Kan sealed every possible exit.

"Let's have a little fun, shall we people!?" He turned the bull toward the stands where thousands of people sit in fear. His eyes locked onto the four of us, and his head cocked to one side.

He flew over to us with the bull in the air. He did an exaggerated sighed. "For ions I've been stuck on this planet and had to work at a stupid eatery. It's time for these mortals to feel my pain… well, my pain is more emotional than physical, but you get the point."

"I thought you were a nice guy." Peter said.

"People can change and you thought wrong." He turned his back to us. "Adios amigos."

I jumped onto his back. Yes, I jumped onto the back of a god. Cancer lost his concentration and we both fell to the ground.

The bull also fell to the ground and its eyes locked onto me in seconds. Cancer used his powers to throw me off of him. He stood and brushed himself off.

"Let's have some fun, mi amigo."

The bull charged me. Cancer sent me flying into the air each time the animal was centimeters away from me.

"Let's have some fun, mi amigo."

"Ole'!" He would say each time. "Ole'!"

He *was* strong. He was strong enough to control my movements and control the bull's mind. This god was crazy. Worst of all, he was crazy strong.

"Cancer! Cut it out!"

"Ole'!" He threw me at his feet.

I looked into his eyes and he laughed. When I glanced passed him, I saw Peter creeping up on him from behind. I smiled as Sofia and Judas tried to get people to safety.

"What, dude? Do you think this is fun?" I said trying to keep Kan's concentration on me.

When he got close enough, Peter fired an arrow and hit Kan directly in the back. The god turned and threw his hands into the air. "Really? You're really trying to fight a *god*?" "All of you will…" His eyes closed unexpectedly and he started to snore.

"What happened to him?" I asked.

"It was a magic sleeping Arrow. He'll be out only for a few hours because he's a god."

We heard sirens approaching. "It's enough time for the authorities to take care of him."

Something grabbed us up and began to fly us away.

"What?"

It was a silhouette. Sofia of course. "Where to now?" I asked.

Judas smiled. "The local police station my good friends. It's where they will take Kan."

Friendship

We went to the police station. At first, the guards wouldn't let us in, but Sofia used her silhouette to change their minds. We walked to Kan's cell. He was in a straight jacket.

"What do you want and why are you here?" he asked us. "You guys knocked me out with magic and hung me out to dry."

"You were going to harm innocent people." I said.

"Cry me a river, dude. A god doesn't concern himself with the safety or harm of mortals."

Judas laughed. "If you're such a mighty god, take off the straight jacket and fly out of here."

"I had a warning from my sister." He said in a low timid voice. "The Elders said that if I expose my powers before mortals again, they'll kill me."

"You're a god." I said, "Gods can't die."

"Zodians can be killed by another Zodian." Sofia said heading for the exit. "Let's leave Cancer to the Zodians."

"Wait!" Kan cried out. "They're going to try to kill me. When they try, I might go insane and try to kill them."

An arrow appeared in Peter's hand. He threw it and hit Kan in the chest. "Go crazy, *amigo*. Nighty night." As Cancer started to snore we left.

We made it back to our room and everyone was exhausted. "Let's get some rest" I said hesitantly.

Sofia rested on the bed next to mine, Peter took the couch, and Judas lied sprawled on the floor. I eventually fell asleep also, but I still didn't have any dreams. Instead of dreams, I had different images coming into my mind.

I saw Leo's deformed animal forms, and I saw the fireplace in the library. I remembered how I was thrown into a fireplace by Leo and teleported. There has been so much magic and strange things happening in my life, and it was all happening so fast. Every occurrence of magic and monsters happened as if it was completely normal in the world. So much was happening around me, and so much of it I didn't understand.

I didn't understand how Cazzner was able to find us. Mercy. She would answer my questions about Leo, Cazzner and everything else.

The whistle she gave me came to my memory. I looked around for the jacket she gave me. I took the whistle from the jacket pocket and sighed. I tried thinking about how I would blow it without waking everyone up. I covered the air hole as an attempt to keep it quiet as I blew. I took my chances. To my surprise, I blew the whistle but it didn't make a sound.

A blue mist formed around the whistle and I dropped it. In the mist came an image of Mercy who was sitting in a chair and reading.

I looked around. "Mercy?" I whispered.

No response.

I grunted and came closer to the image. "Mercy!" I whispered louder.

She dropped the book and looked around until she saw me.

I waved and she raised an eyebrow.

"Cyrus? What's wrong?"

"I blew the whistle because I need help. I have a question?"

"Okay." She adjusted in her chair. "I'm listening."

"Leo's son took me into a library, and I met Leo there. His daughter said that his son brought me there because I broke into his house."

"Okay." Mercy said with no effort.

"I didn't break into his house, but I dreamt that I was in his house."

She tapped her finger on her lips. "It's simple. Sometimes the children of the Zodians have dreams that will predict the future, or sometimes what they think is a dream may be actually reality. The dream you had with the cave was not a dream but rather, it was real. You did go to Calvin's house. Understand?"

"Okay."

"Yeah." I said. "I do."

"Any other questions?" She asked.

"Yes I have many more."

No, she said, only one more.

You're the daughter of Virgo, so how can you be a witch?"

She bit her lip. "Witch Greta, that is all I can say about that, no one can know the rest."

"Thanks for the help," I said.

She smiled at me, but I could tell it was forced. "You're welcome. Oh, and don't worry. The dreams tend to go away as time goes by." The cloud disappeared into the whistle on the floor leaving a rotten cheesy smell.

I fell asleep, and just like she said, I didn't have any dreams.

When everyone finally woke up, it was late night. We all crowded around the small old TV. The picture was fuzzy and every channel was in Spanish.

"Wait," Judas said, "why are we watching TV? Shouldn't we start for Africa now? I mean, the sooner the better."

"Remember what Witch Greta said?" I asked.

"No," he said. "Was it important?"

"Yes, someone is going to die in the desert." Sofia said.

"There's no way to avoid the desert though." Judas responded.

There was a knock at the door, and Peter stood to answer it. "You do have a point. She didn't say how that someone would die, so we can't rule anything out."

He opened the door.

I shook my head. "Don't tell me we came this far to quit."

"We're not quitting." Sofia assured me. "We just need to-"

There was a thud, and the three of us looked over to the door. Peter laid limp on the floor, and a man entered the room. He looked like a normal man who was dressed in all black and wore a bandana over his mouth... but he had green smoke oozing from his body.

The smoke filled the room and Sofia hit the ground.

I looked at Judas, and he looked at me.

"What is this?"

He shrugged and smelled the air. "Smells like a..." He tapped his foot. "It's like a magical sleeping powder."

"Why aren't you affected?" Green smoke was going in and out of his nostrils. "Probably because I'm dead? What about you?"

"I don't know. I- wait! What do you mean you're dead!?"

"Let's not have a casual conversation when there is a suspicious person standing at the door."

It wore a gas mask. It slowly walked over to us saying, "Dang children."

"Let's go." Judas grabbed Peter and headed for the window.

I picked Sofia up in my arms and ran to the window. I looked back at the thing in the room. It was staring at me. I turned quickly back to the window again. I jumped out feeling the nighttime air rush in my ears. I somehow landed on my feet without hurting Sofia or me.

Judas stood in front of me. "Cyrus, your brother isn't waking up. We need some kind of incent."

I laid Sofia on the ground beside Peter. "I don't have anything. I sat down on a nearby bench and looked at Peter and Sofia.

They'll be awake soon." Judas assured me.

Hey, what did you mean about being dead?"

"Come on, Cyrus!"

"I am dead." He said casually.

I nodded. "That's what I thought you said "I never knew that about you… that you're dead I mean. I guess that just never came up in conversation. Do you have any hobbies?"

"I died in 1998."

I shut up and listened.

"From what I know, someone dug up my grave and put the Aries Gem on me. I don't know who did it, or why they chose me. I'll stay alive so long as I have the Gem."

"So you look dead because you are, or because of the Gem?"

"The Gem makes me look... weird. But I don't care. This thing keeps me alive."

I remembered my dream and the gravestone. "You were born in 1844."

"Yeah," he said. "Judeas Vincewell was my name." He sighed and smiled. "Man I was awesome. Judeas Vincewell, successful child prodigy. Special skills: piano, violin, art, doctoring, and my favorite, martial arts."

"You okay?" I asked.

He sniffed like he was crying. His voice was shaky. "I'm

"How could you live for that long?" I asked.

There was a very long pause before he answered. "In the past I worked for one of the Zodians. You have to be alive to serve them."

"If you don't mind my asking, which one?"

I didn't get a response.

"Do you remember anything?"

"I remember *everything*." His gaze looked distant.

"You okay?" I asked again.

He simply nodded. "When I was resurrected I was reincarnated in this body." His hands formed fists. "You take what you get. Sofia helped me enroll into Garamond, and I was there ever since."

"How long have you known Sofia?"

No answer.

Fine.

"Why wasn't I affected by the smoke?" I asked changing the subject.

"You tell me."

We heard a groaning. Peter and Sofia were slowly waking up.

Sofia sighed. "How long has it been?"

"Maybe a little over an hour."

"So what happened back in the room?" I asked Peter once he was fully awake.

"Jebediah Simons." Peter grunted. "We were pals for a while. We did jobs for… people. He wanted to go rouge so they left him to rot. Now, he trying to take his revenge out on me."

"Instead of going after the people who left him to rot?" I paused and thought. Did Peter used to work for the Zodians too?

"I'm sorry all of you got caught in this."

"Don't worry about it," I said. "It's fine. We can handle him."

"Let's just get going." Judas said. It's better if we travel at night now."

"Judas, come with me." Sofia motioned to him.

"Cyrus you and Peter go on ahead of us." The two of them stood under a street light. They were engulfed by a silhouette and then they disappeared.

I faced Peter. "We have to walk don't we?"

"After you." He gestured.

I folded my arms and he laughed before walking away.

My legs tired out, but Peter kept his stride. By now, the only lights we had were the street lights. If you have never walked in the dark before, then you don't know what fear really is. Every little noise keeps you on edge, and every person walking by you is automatically a threat.

I felt a cool breeze on the back of my neck and I jumped. I turned and was face to face with a silhouette that was standing on its feet. I waved my hand in front of it then called Peter. He shrugged, and it extended its body towards us. We climbed on its back, and it flew us away.

After days and days of flying, resting in hotels, and flying more, we made it. We landed at an area that was completely bare. There was nothing behind us for miles and water ahead of us for miles. We were at the Strait of Gibraltar.

Judas and Sofia were already there sleeping. Peter and I crashed beside them and slept.

Around midday we all woke up talking about what happened to us. Not one time did Sofia or Judas say what they talked about or why they separated from us. They only talked about what happened to them in the room. After we were done talking, we faced the water.

Sofia breathed in. "Salt water."

"So." I said. "What's bad about salt water."

"This water is contaminated." She said. "It has a poison that effects immortals, mystical powers, and especially wielders or keepers of the Zodiac Gems."

"So the Elders put the poison in the water?" I asked.

"Yep." Peter said. "We need to fly over it."

"We can't." Judas said sadly. "There'll be a force field around the area."

I had the perfect idea. "I know what to do. We'll build a raft. Then I'll take off my watch and leave it with you. I will use the raft to float to the other side. When I reach the Atlas Mountains I'll send some kind of signal and then you guys can…"

"Are you insane?" Peter yelled. "You can't go on a raft in the Strait of Gibraltar! You'll die!"

"Relax." I said. "I know what I'm doing. Trust me."

Peter sighed. "Just be careful."

The wooden raft was built. It even had a paddle to match. I was ready. I took off my watch. A red scar lined along the area the watch was. I handed the Gem to Peter and faced the water. "So long. Pray that I make it. I promise I'll find a way for you guys to pass the force field."

I took a deep breath and got on the raft. It floated away. The only thing I could think about was the others being afraid that I would die.

I saw Sofia holding on to Judas's shoulder. Peter had his sunglasses off. He was watching me carefully. I felt something warm inside of me.

The raft glowed green for a brief second then the glow went away. I felt the water and it was cold. Not just cold, but freezing cold. I started to form ice sickles on my nose. My skin started to turn light blue. I was coughing and wanted to turn around, but I couldn't. The raft kept on moving forward. I tried to use the paddle to stop, but it froze. I floated around puking and moaning, until I saw something in the water.

It was a penny. Only it wasn't an ordinary penny. It had Abraham Lincoln on it, but he didn't look the same. He wasn't turned to the side instead he was facing forward. His beard was cut short and he wore a fez. I picked it up but I had no feeling in my hands now. Everything was starting to freeze on my body. I felt doomed.

Death in the Desert

"Thanks for finding that for me." A voice said from behind me.

It was a cat. The same green cat Mercy had in her car. "Can I have my coin back?"

My jaw dropped. "Y-you can talk!?" I sneezed. My lips were almost frozen shut.

It rolled its eyes. Then it transformed into a man with black hair, a mechanic's jumpsuit, and had oil marks on his hands and face. "I'm Patrick." He said to me. *You* may remember me from your little ride with Mercy von Tomb?"

"Yeah." I said. "Why were you a cat?" My lips were barely parting to speak.

"I disobeyed one of the Sacred Twelve so they turned me into a cat. I can only transform into my human self if I'm around a Zodian's child.

Peter handed him the coin with frozen fingers. "Thank you."

"Why didn't you transform when we were in the car?" My body continued to freeze more.

"Because I didn't feel like it." He said.

"Why is your penny different from other pennies." I couldn't feel my lips now.

"Because that's how Abraham Lincoln used to look." He said. "Scorpio wanted him to lead an army against Japan. Abraham refused, so he was cursed. His beard could never be cut and his death would be public around a lot of people during an important event in his life. Now the big hat was his own idea."

"Do you have any powers?" My lips finally froze.

"Like what, those Gems? Oh no, but I can help you." He walked behind the raft. The cold didn't seem to bother him. He inhaled then exhaled.

The raft took off at top speed. I nearly fell off. The paddle flew backward. My eyelids were being blown back by the wind. I wasn't blue any more, the ice sickles were slowly melting, my sickness passed, and my lips thawed.

In minutes I saw land. "Land." I said to myself. "Land."

The raft caught onto the edge of the Strait. I was sent flying into a cactus. "Ow!" I yelled. I looked at the Strait and saw someone coming walking on the waters.

It was Patrick, and he had Sofia, Judas, and Peter with him. They were walking on the water together. Lucky them. They got to perform something that hasn't been performed in several thousand years. Walking on water. I wish I 'd waited.

Patrick smiled. "I found your friends."

The three of them ran over to me. Peter smiled. "Looks like you didn't die." He helped me up off the ground.

Patrick clapped his hands. "Come now, the Atlas Mountains awaits. Follow me my new friends."

Patrick brought us to three camels with water and supplies on each. Judas and Sofia rode together, Peter and I rode together and Patrick rode the other one. The three camels took off quick, and I noticed why. They weren't real animal camels. They were machines disguised as camels. I could tell because smoke was coming out of it. Then I thought about something more serious. I knew the others had to be thinking about it to. The prophecy. One of us would die in the desert, but who?

We literally went through the Atlas Mountains in no time. It was like a phantom experience. We were on the other side of the mountain.

"The Sahara Desert is next." Patrick said. "Keep moving."

While we were riding I realized something else. Patrick could go in the water. Sofia said no mystical being could enter or go near the water. So how could Patrick? I had more questions to think of, but no time. Something went wrong.

Patrick's Mechanical Camel fell into a sink hole. We all stopped and jumped down to help.

Patrick looked up at us. "We're near natives. We need to leave now." He jumped from the hole. He did an impressive aerial flip and landed perfectly on his feet. "Come on."

"What about your camel?" Judas asked.

"Forget it." Patrick said. "You four need to go through the desert I don't. Just keep traveling. You have a map. Use it."

"No." Sofia said. "Please come with us."

Patrick grunted. "Fine. I'll come if you can get my M.C. out of the hole."

"M.C.?" I asked.

"Mechanical Camel." He said. "Now please get it out."

I held out my hand toward the camel, but it didn't move. "Why isn't Aquarius working?"

"Here." Peter handed me the Gem. "You forgot to get it back when we got over the Strait.

"Oh, right." I put it on and it felt good. I used the Gem to move the camel out of the hole.

"Let's go, quickly." Patrick said nervously.

We all climbed on our camels and rode off. We rode for hours and hours. By midnight Patrick said we were fifty miles from Egypt. We stopped to rest. Patrick switched the camels to Guard Mode and we all went to sleep. We had to sleep on sand, and we were forced to feel the cold night air.

Evidently, the desert makes many noises at night. Scratching, wet footsteps, groaning – these are just some of the noises you will hear when you are sleeping in the middle of a desert that is absolutely freezing at night. Not only will you hear these noises, but you will also have a spear chucked at you.

A spear was chucked at me.

It wisped by my ear, and I yelled in order to wake everyone.

From the darkness glowed many sets of pure white eyes. Men with painted faces and spears came into view.

One wore a headdress and held a bronze tip spear. He yelled something in his language and the other men began to raise their spears and shields as they circled around us and chanted. In seconds African Pygmies surrounded us.

"I thought Pygmies lived in forests?" I said.

"They do." Sofia commented. "Apparently these don't."

One of the Pygmies stood forward. He had a bronze tip spear. He spoke, but we all shook our heads to say we didn't understand. He kept speaking different language.

"Trespassers!" He finally said in English. "Your lucky I have been to America and various countries when I was a boy, or else you would have been killed for not understanding! This is our home! Leave or be killed!"

"No." Patrick said. "We need to get to Alexandria, Egypt. So move out of our way!"

The Pygmy threw his spear at Patrick. Patrick dived on the ground. The spear hit the sand with a loud thud. "You missed! Short stack!"

The Pygmy yelled and they all threw spears at Patrick.

"Run." Patrick whispered to us. "I'll be fine."

We climbed on the Camels and rode off fast. I turned back and saw Patrick being surrounded by the Pygmies. I looked closer and saw him being stabbed to death.

We journeyed several hours away before we eventually stopped to rest. Sofia sighed. "Someone would die in the desert. That someone was Patrick."

"He gave up his life," Peter added, "to save ours. He barely knew us."

We all had the hardest time trying to fall asleep. I closed my eyes and dreamed that Patrick's body was being buried in the sand.

Our Destination

Judas was the first to wake up. He said he went back to the place Patrick was killed. "There was no trace of him or the Pygmies." He said. "The Pygmies must have taken him with them."

"No." I said.

"Last night, I dreamt Patrick's death. I also saw him being buried in the sand."

"At least the worse part of the prophecy is gone." Sofia said. "The part of the witch's vision about the friends' must have been Kan or Lance. The person finding out their true self is solved also." She looked at me and smiled. "Judas and I found out the legend part."

"Who's the legend?" I asked.

"Peter," said Judas.

"When Sofia and I left you and Peter, everyone we saw was talking about him. The news called him a legend for fighting Kan."

"Sweet." Peter said with enthusiasm. "I'm a legend. Now the best part of the prophecy. All of us will become knights."

"We better get moving."

I hopped on the *Camel* and the others did too. We pushed the speed meter up to *Dangerously Fast*. It *was* dangerously fast. We rode until the camels ran hot. By that time, we were near the border of Egypt. We left the camels and walked on until we reached the border. We each breathed in simultaneously then stepped across into Egypt. We looked and everything was different.

Children ran around playing games. Adult men walked with spears in their hands, and adult women walked with vases on the top of their heads. Merchants pointed to their merchandise and smiled. One merchant in particular stood out.

She was knitting a robe that Santa Claus could wear. She was old and wore a simple red dashiki. A blue rag covered her hair. She sat in an African wooden chair.

Her smile was receiving. "I'm Nita, she who hates the Zodian goddess Virgo the most."

Sofia sat on the ground beside her. "Why? You seem like a nice woman. I can't seem to think you would have any hate in your heart."

A tear came out of the woman's eye. "She killed my husband." She paused.

Sofia patted her on the back. "Say no more."

The widow managed a smile. "Thank you. Virgo wanted me to tell you that her and three other Elders are waiting for you. The Temple is not far from this place. Be careful." We walked away leaving the poor woman to her knitting.

We tried to buy some camels, but the merchant didn't speak English and he wouldn't take our money. So we stole the camels while his back was turned. We didn't have any water but we would worry about that later. We quietly made it away from the merchant's market. We stopped for a quick break.

I looked at Sofia. "What's wrong?"

"Nothing," she said, "it's just that, I told Patrick he had to come with us. So his death was my fault. He didn't want to come with us."

"No it wasn't your fault." I tried to sound reassuring. "He offered to risk his life. He didn't have to."

"I'm sorry to interrupt your therapy session," Judas said sarcastically. "I would like to inform you that *gargantuan* here lost the map." He pointed at Peter.

Peter threw up his hands. "The wind did it. Wait, I'm not a *gargantuan*."

Judas scoffed. "Please, you have muscles on your muscles! Plus, those muscles have muscles!"

"Shouldn't we be worried about the map?" I asked.

"It's okay," Sofia said pulling out Cazzner's journal.
"Wait a minute." She paused for five minutes. "The Temple of Zodia isn't in Alexandria." She held up the journal. "It's in Cairo."

"Well the *gargantuan* thinks we should get a move on." Peter said.

"Gargantuan be right." Judas taunted again. "First I would like to point out that, there is no more water! I'm parched here!"

"Look." I pointed toward an oasis in the distance.

Judas jumped off the camel. "Water!" He ran to the oasis. But it ended up being a mirage. "No water." He said.

We all looked up as a huge wind blew down on us. A helicopter lowered itself beside us. A familiar looking girl stepped out with a familiar looking cat.

She smiled. "Patrick, I think we found them." Her long red hair blew upward. "If you want to go to the Temple then come on." We climbed on the gold helicopter and watched as we lifted off the ground into the cold air.

"I bet you're are wondering how Patrick survived?" Mercy said as we took our seats.

Sofia folded her arms. "No."

"Well I'll tell you anyway. The Zodian made him immortal just in case they needed him." She set him down and he turned into his human self."

"Aloha." He said adjusting his clothes. "Did you miss me?"

Sofia ran and gave him a hug.

"Don't worry." Patrick said letting go of her. "I'm fine."

Mercy clapped her hands. "Fredrick faster if you will."

"Yes, Madame Mercy." Fredrick sat up straight. "Right away." The helicopter flew faster.

We didn't say or do much while we were waiting. We just looked out window. The whole time I was thinking about how the Temple was going to look. Just a few days ago I was in Callisto bored out of my mind. Now I was on my way to a place I wanted to see my entire life.

"We're above the Temple." Mercy said. She threw us parachutes to put on.

"There's nothing down there but sand." Judas yelled over the helicopter blades looking out the window.

"Not exactly." Mercy pushed Judas out the door.

Judas fell out screaming. "Heeeelp!"

I jumped out with Peter behind me. "Hold on Judas!"

Sofia flew down on her shadow. "Hi." She flew to Judas and opened his parachute. Peter and I did the same when we got low enough to the ground.

We both tumbled a couple of times then landed on our backs. Sofia and Judas were kneeling on the ground. Peter and I walked up to them. "What are you doing?" Peter asked.

Two skeletons rose behind Judas. It was Gertrude and Garner. "Digging. This may take a while sonny."

After two days of digging the skeletons were finished. Gertrude and Garner returned to the After Life. There was a deep enormous hole in the ground. We looked down inside and saw numerous lights shining brighter than stars. Each of us looked at the other and knew what we needed to do. Without hesitation, we all slid down the hole. It felt like we were falling for days before we hit the bottom. We stood and looked around in amazement. "The Temple of Zodia."

We are Given Our Tasks

We walked around several hours before we found a huge door. There were no knobs or handles on the door. It was as wide as a football field. Peter pushed on the door with all his might. His face turned red with exhaustion. For a second nothing happened. Then the door opened slowly.

We all walked through the door at the same time. Everything was awesome. Large tapestries hung on the wall. Each portrayed the different Zodian in hieroglyphic style (except Cancer) above a bronze fireplace. The white marble floors showed our reflections perfectly. The black onyx walls sparkled with blue glittering diamonds. The lighting had no source. It just existed.

We walked onward and found two hallways. One leading right, the other leading left. "Which way?" I asked.

Judas scratched his head. "I say we go…"

As we looked from left to right, suddenly the wall directly in front of us moved. It slowly slid open from the middle. We each looked at each other and instinctively held hands. Judas smiled. "… that way." He pointed forward.

We all exchanged looks then stepped inside slowly. When we walked in, I nearly fainted. In front of us were twelve large, majestic thrones. My heart nearly stopped. In four of the thrones sat four of the Zodiac gods. I remembered them from the books I read about Zodiac gods.

There was a throne made out of stone that showed its age by the cracks it bore; on it sat the Zodian god Taurus. The throne next to him, made out of vines was Virgo, she really *was* beautiful. Three seats down from her was someone not really on a throne. It was an oversized pet bed that was made out of straws of hay. Sagittarius lifted his head and his horsehair stood on end. The second to last throne sat the person I feared the most. Aquarius slouched on his metal throne as he played with a tiny metal ball.

Taurus stood, and straightened his white toga. He walked toward us with thunderous steps. "Welcome!" His voice was booming. "Welcome to the Temple of Zodia!" He turned to Sofia and smiled as he put his thumb under her chin and smiled. "And how are you, Samantha?"

For the first time in my life, I saw Sofia blush. It was certainly a sight to see.

"I'm fine, daddy."

Judas jumped. "Taurus the Zodian god of Strength is your dad?"

"Your name is *Samantha*?" I asked after him.

She punched my arm without remorse. "Never call me that!"

Taurus sighed in amusement then hummed. "How did you find this place, children?"

"My disrespectful daughter." Virgo shouted from her throne. "I know we're not supposed to tell our children where we live, and I didn't. I'll punish her later."

"There will be none of that, Virgo." Sagittarius said softly. "Children will be children. Let each be that which his soul gives. You can't change that."

"I thought you were the Zodian god of Archery, not poetry." Virgo taunted.

Sagittarius sighed.

"Hush!" Taurus stomped back to his seat. "What do you need, young people? Why are you here?"

"We want to find all your Gems." I said excited.

Peter put his hand on my shoulder to calm me down. "As you know your honor, the power Gems can be used to destroy mankind."

"And?" Virgo said without enthusiasm. "How can we trust that you will retrieve the Gems *and* bring them back to us?"

"I trained that one myself; we can trust him." Sagittarius stated as he pointed to Peter.

"And *clearly* we can trust your daughter. But, the other two *are* questionable I suppose." Taurus said.

Aquarius had yet to say a word or look in our direction.

"No, we can't trust my daughter Mercy." Virgo snapped. "Remember Sagittarius, she nearly killed your son over a Gem they ended up losing."

"Losing, your husband took it!" Sofia yelled at Virgo.

"He *retrieved* it." Virgo yelled back.

190

"He did no-"

"Nevertheless," Sagittarius interrupted, "we can still trust Mercy. My son Wilson needed to be taught a lesson. I admit he is unruly in nature."

Virgo smirked. "Like you said. 'let each be that which his soul gives'."

"What about that boy?" The centaur god said ignoring her. He pointed to Judas.

Judas looked around. "Me? You can trust me. I can be trusted."

Sofia shook her head. "We did *not* take a long, journey here to be denied. So stop it!" She yelled. "We can all be trusted."

"You really are your father's child." The goddess observed. "You both have the same temper."

Taurus pointed at Aquarius. "What do *you* think?"

The metal ball in Aquarius's hand disappeared. He scratched his gray hair then lifted his hand. He didn't say a word, but the Elders all nodded to signal they understand.

"Very well." Taurus snapped his fingers.

The sound nearly caused me to go deaf. The noise swirled all around the room and in seconds, the other

Zodians appeared on their thrones. I was overwhelmed with joy to see them. All the Zodians were now seated before us (except Cancer).

Capricorn with his goat head, Pisces on his throne made of water, Aries with his scythe, Scorpio holding a flaming trident, Leo in lion form, Gemini on a throne made out of shadows. Then the most unusual Elder. Libra, he was wearing a knight's armor. One side of the armor was white the other side was black. The mask on his armor covered his face. Floating above his head was the universe. He stood upright and raised his right hand. I was so excited I started to tear up.

"May the meeting of the Elders of Zodia come to order." He sat back down on his throne.

"Can we hurry this up?" Aries asked. "My helpers usually eat the new guests that come to the After Life. I need to get back as soon as possible."

"I agree." Gemini groaned. "I have a nail appointment soon."

"Hush now, both of you." Pisces said. He sounded as if he was gurgling water. "This meeting must be of great importance to gather us all at once."

"We get it!" Scorpio hissed and he caught fire. "Just shut up! I have people to burn!"

I leaned over to Peter. "Is he who I think he is?"

"No." Peter replied. "You are thinking of his son. Scorpio's *only* son. Thank goodness."

"Elders please," Sagittarius said. "These young people before us have volunteered to find our Gems for us. The Gems will be in good hands with them. They are trustworthy."

"Again with the poetry, Sag." Virgo said.

"Let's just give them the map." Pisces said.

"The map?" I asked. "You have a map that shows where the Gems are located? You have a map, but you won't retrieve the Gems yourselves?"

All the Zodians gasped and stared at me. "How dare you?" They all said simultaneously (except for Aquarius).

"What my friend Cyrus is trying to ask is, what might be preventing you from getting the Gems, your honors?" Peter asked trying to protect me.

"We became distracted with earthly pleasures when we lived among the mortals. Also, we were always busy." Aries said. "We each have our own job to do. As you can imagine, the After Life can be messy."

"I have to take care of the ea-r-r-r-rth." Capricorn said.

Gemini lifted her hand. "Tick tock, tick tock. Let's give them the map already. I don't want to be late for my manicure."

"You should get a pedicure instead." Virgo taunted. Gemini looked at her. They both started laughing.

Libra stood. "Very well. You four, we shall-"

"Wait." A voice said.

All the Elders turned and looked at Aquarius in surprised. He stood from his throne and walked to the center of the room.

"H-he spoke? Aries said.

"He has never spoken before." Sagittarius looked with amazement.

"My fellow Zodians," Aquarius continued, "I have spoken on this day to tell a secret that I have kept for 12 years."

"This must be a good secret." Virgo said under her breath.

My watch began to rattle and I was pulled to the center of the room with him.

He placed his hand on my shoulder and we faced the gods. "This boy is… he is…" He shook his head. "This boy is my… my son."

"What!" All the Elders said.

I looked back at my friends in surprise. They shrugged their shoulders.

Aquarius waved his hand to get everyone's attention again. "I never spoke of this before because I failed to take care of him. It is high time I take full responsibility for him."

No one said a word so he continued to talk.

"I believe you should allow these four to journey and collect the Gems. They are mortals; therefore, they are imperfect. Nonetheless, they were brave enough to travel here and meet with us face to face. We must have faith in them."

I scratched my head. "For the record I didn't know about this until just now so…" I said.

The Elders were still silent. Then Leo roared. "Well your boy was in my son's home."

"I'm aware." Aquarius said with a smile. "Although he didn't understand how he got there. Until a certain girl named Mercy von Tomb explained it to him. She answered his questions so he understood more of what was happening in his life."

Virgo flipped her hair. "Fine, maybe my daughters not *all* bad. She's just disrespectful."

"There is voting to be done, is there not?" Libra stood again. "A verdict is to be reached. Will we allow these four mortals to go on a vast adventure throughout the earth to retrieve and return our Gems?"

Murmurs filled the room for several minutes before Aries stood. He removed his hood. "The verdict, my friend..." He turned to Libra.

"It shall be."

"Meeting is adjourned. We meet back here in one hour to give them the map."

The Zodians left the room one by one.

Aquarius gave me a rather loving smile. "Well done, my son. Come we must speak."

"O-okay... *dad.*" Of all of the Zodians to be the son of, I was the son of the god whose Gem I got. Ironic.

My newly discovered dad decided to show me his bedroom (which, was sadly next to Virgo's room). He told me that the rooms were more of a relaxation place for them. Apparently, gods don't need sleep. The doorknob turned itself and he pointed inside. I stepped through the doorway and my dad followed in. Everything was metal, the windows and furniture included. The only exception was the bed linen.

I looked at him. "Why is everything you have metal?"

"I am the Zodian god of Magnetism."

"Isn't it a bit too much though?"

"Personally, I love the décor of metal. It is who I'am." He sat down in a chair. "Sit anywhere you like."

I sat on the bed. "Why have you never spoken before?"

He shrugged casually and clenched his fist. "I was ashamed. I couldn't take care of my own son. I was so distracted. I just stopped speaking."

"I was born twelve years ago." I reminded him. "Aries said you've never spoken before."

"Correct. I've never spoken because all the Elders would just argue. I never saw an opportunity or had a need to speak. So I didn't."

"Where is my mother and who is she?"

He was caught off guard by the question but answered nonetheless. "When a mortal has the child of a Zodian, the mortal will die."

"Why?" I heard my heart break.

"To protect our existence. We can't have mortals speaking about us. But I loved your mortal mother very much, which is not allowed. So you see, I have many reasons not to speak."

In a low shaky sad voice, I asked "Why is Edward von Tomb an exception?" I was fighting back tears.

"He worked for Scorpio. Virgo met him, and they had a child. Still yet, Scorpio kept von Tomb immortal so that he can continue to serve him and run the prison."

"So everyone else gets to die because they don't serve a Zodiac god.?" I blinked back more tears.

He sighed and a drawer pulled out. He pointed and I walked to the drawer. I reached inside and pulled out a picture.

"She's your mother." She had long black hair and blue eyes.

"Is she in the After Life?" I held the picture in my hand close to my chest.

"Yes, she's in paradise."

"Do you visit her?" I had to keep fighting the tears.

When he didn't answer I asked again.

"Yes, Aries allows me to visit her every day."

"Aries is my uncle, right?"

"Yes. And he told me all about your death experience."

"Who was it that killed me?" I asked.

"I'm not the Zodian god of Death. I'm sorry."

"Do the other Elders know you and Aries are brothers?" I still had the picture in my hand.

"No, there is no reason for them to know. It must stay a secret for now."

"When we first started our journey, you sent me a text saying you wanted your Gem back." I said.

"Text?" He asked. "I don't even own a cellular phone. What phone received the text?"

"Kan… uh, Cancer gave me the phone. A while after the text, the phone self-destructed."

"Lancaster," Aquarius said calmly. "The phone came from *Cancer* so he must have played a prank on you. He is known for many mischievous things."

"Right." I scratched my head. "What is my real name?"

The god nodded. "Lancaster. Your mother named you that because her name was Landra. It seemed close enough to hers."

I had my mother's name. I put the picture in my pocket. I didn't think Aquarius would miss it.

"Now, onto more important business- the Gem.

"Let me guess, I can only keep the Gem if I use it for good and not evil."

My dad sighed. "Yes, you took the words right out of my mouth. Do not use it unnecessarily." Then he held up the scroll and scepter I had days ago.

"How did you get those?"

"If you don't mind I would like to keep them." He didn't answer how he got them.

"Sure, as long as the scroll isn't right."

I noted that he didn't comment.

"Why did everyone besides me know who I really was?"

The metal cuckoo clock rung. My dad handed me a metal ball. "A parting gift." He stood and motioned for me to leave.

As I walked out the door, Virgo was just coming out her room.

She looked at me and smirked. "You're not as noble as you think you are."

I ignored her, but she put her hand on my shoulder and stared into my eyes. "You have such pretty eyes. They twinkle like the stars that light our Temple. But I haven't forgotten what you did."

"Virgo, that's enough!" My dad came out the room.

I walked with my dad and didn't look back.

"Don't mind her, Lancaster."

We walked to the throne room and I stood beside my friends as Aquarius gathered in a circle with the other Zodians. Virgo was the last to enter the circle.

The gap between Sagittarius and Taurus made the circle they formed incomplete.

Catching fire, Scorpio said "we need Cancer to complete the circle.!"

"Obviously, hot head." Gemini quipped.

"Don't call me that!"

"Watch your tone!"

"Hush!" Sagittarius looked over to Libra. "We do need Cancer." Libra shook his head yes.

"Gemini? Shall we?"

"We don't have much of a choice do we." A silhouette left her and came back just as fast as it left.

Kan fell out of the shadow. He pulled the earphones out of his ears. "Hey!" He looked at Gemini. "Sis?" He looked around. "Am I home? I am actually home. Thanks!"

"Shut up, little brother." Gemini said. "We need you for once."

Cancer smiled. "Sweet! What are we doing?"

"We are making the map to reveal where our Gems are located." Taurus said.

"Just stand in your place and shut up." Virgo yelled.

"Yes ma'am!"

All the Elders stretched out their hands to the center. A rainbow of colors appeared. Then Libra moved to the center of the rainbow. The universe on top of his head started to spin quickly and grew larger. It created a whirlwind that blew us to the floor. Then it slowly stopped and shrunk back down to its normal size again. The Zodians dropped their out stretched hands and a piece of paper fell to the ground.

Libra retrieved the paper. "This is the map that shows the location of the remaining Gems."

The map was handed to me.

He turned to so Sofia. "When a Gem is found you, must return it to this Temple by way of shadow. Do you understand?"

Sofia nodded shyly. "I do."

"I'd also advise you all to be cautious. Not all of the Gems lie undiscovered." Libra warned us.

Sagittarius trotted over to us. "I will show you the way out." We followed.

He took us to a gold airplane on the backside of the Temple. Aquarius made sure everything was working properly. "Please make sure you don't spill or break anything on this plane."

"Yeah make sure of that." Virgo told us. "Solid gold airplanes don't grow on trees."

All the other Zodians walked out to say goodbye. Cancer jumped around happily thanking us. Taurus gave Sofia a hug, Judas was talking to Aries about a part-time job in the After Life, and Peter was talking to Capricorn just to hear his voice. Then you had me. Aquarius shook my hand then gave me a hug.

Peter, Judas, Sofia, and I boarded the plane. We took our seats when Kan hopped aboard too. "Let me take you to your destination, amigos. It's the least I could do after all the trouble I've caused."

"Oh no!" Virgo yelled. "There is no way I'm allowing *you* to take *my* plane! There is no way! You better hop back off or else…" A silhouette's hand covered Virgo's mouth.

Gemini laughed. "Go ahead little brother."

The other Zodians nodded in approval with hopes Cancer can amend some of his wrongs.

He got in the pilot chair. "Now how do you start this thing? Cancer started pushing buttons. Oh wait this is the intercom. Maybe this button?" We started flying up slowly.

We all waved good-bye to the Elders once more. I looked over at Sofia. "You okay?" I asked.

She wiped a tear from her eye and smiled. "Never better." She punched my arm and I smiled.

"Good." Judas said putting his arm around her. "Now let's get the first Gem."

Peter laughed. "Before you three start anything you're going to enroll in school."

"Great." Judas moaned.

Sofia smiled. "It really is."

I smiled too. I pulled out the picture of my mother. "I love you." I said looking at the picture. "I love you." Then, I fell asleep dreaming about my mom for the first time.

The Journey Continues

Kaitlyn McKnight

Thank you for your support!

COMING SOON
Zodiac Saga 2: The Search for the Gems

www.ingramcontent.com/pod-product-compliance
Lightning Source LLC
Chambersburg PA
CBHW031951130726
47905CB00009BA/3005